CHRISTMAS CLOCHES AND CORPSES

A Ghostly Fashionista Mystery

Gayle Leeson

Grace Abraham Publishing

D1214587

Gayle Leeson
Grace Abraham Publishing
A Division of Washington Cooper, Inc.
13335 Holbrook St.
Bristol, Virginia 24202

Publisher's Note: This is a work of fiction. Names, characters, places, and incidents are a product of the author's imagination. Locales and public names are sometimes used for atmospheric purposes. Any resemblance to actual people, living or dead, or to businesses, companies, events, institutions, or locales is completely coincidental.

Book Layout ©2017 BookDesignTemplates.com

Ordering Information:
Quantity sales. Special discounts are available on quantity purchases by corporations, associations, and others. For details, contact the "Special Sales Department" at the address above.

Christmas Cloches and Corpses/ Gayle Leeson -- 1st ed.
ISBN 978-1-7320195-5-3

Also by Gayle Leeson

A Ghostly Fashionista Mystery Series

Designs on Murder

Perils and Lace

Christmas Cloches and Corpses

Down South Café Mystery Series

The Calamity Café

Silence of the Jams

Honey-Baked Homicide

Apples and Alibis

Fruit Baskets and Holiday Caskets

Kinsey Falls Chick-Lit Series

Hightail It to Kinsey Falls

Putting Down Roots in Kinsey Falls

Sleighing It in Kinsey Falls

Writing as Amanda Lee

Writing as Gayle Trent

For Tim, Lianna, and Nicholas

Fashion is the armor to survive the reality of everyday life.

–BILL CUNNINGHAM

Chapter One

I couldn't have been in a more embarrassing predicament if I'd planned it out. There I stood in my workroom—atelier, if you prefer—with my arms up over my head and a black lace dress hanging from my nose to mid-thigh. The dress was stuck.

Jasmine, my cat, apparently found the situation amusing. She stood on her hind legs and tried to swipe at the hem.

"Jazzy, no! Stop it!" If she got her claws into the lace and tore this dress, I'd never get it fixed in time for my client to pick it up this afternoon.

At that moment, my best friend, Max, popped in to see what was going on. "Good thing you've got great gams since you're showing them off like that."

"It's not my intention to show off anything," I said. "I'm trying to get this dress back off."

"Let me see if I can help." Max got closer to me and began to flutter her arms like a giant bird in a mauve flapper dress.

"What are you doing?"

"I thought I'd see if I could create a breeze." She continued fluttering.

Since Max was a ghost, she couldn't physically help me remove the dress. At least, she was providing an interesting distraction for Jazzy.

"Could you please use my phone to text Connie and ask her to come in here?" While Max couldn't touch things, she was a whiz with electronics.

Connie's shop, Delightful Home, was across the hall from mine. Shops on Main also housed Everything Paper, Antiquated Editions, and Jason Logan's photography studio. There was another space, but it was currently vacant.

"Yes. I'll text Connie." She giggled. "You kinda look like Mata Hari. Are you sure you wouldn't rather have me text Jason instead?"

Jason was my boyfriend. He was the last person I'd want to see me looking this stupid, and Max knew it.

"Please hurry," I said.

"He's on his way."

"Good try. He's taking holiday portraits of a family at their home in Bristol today."

I'd barely gotten the words out of my mouth when Connie came into the workroom. "Oh, my goodness! You are in a fix! How did you even manage to text me?"

"It wasn't easy," I said.

"We're taking the dress off, right?" she asked.

"Yes. The material is so delicate, I can't get the dress back over my head without risking a tear."

Jazzy's interest in the dress had been rekindled upon Connie's arrival. I turned a pleading gaze on Max.

"Oh, right, darling. Sorry." She moved over to where Jazzy could see her and then walked over to the other side of the room. Jazzy followed on her heels, as Max spoke to her affectionately.

Although Connie couldn't see or hear Max, Jazzy could; and she adored the ghostly fashionista.

Connie helped me ease the dress over my head. I was glad I'd worn a decent bra and panties today, even though it didn't help alleviate my embarrassment much. Still, Connie was terrific—she turned away and waited for me to slip back into my fifties-style A-line blue dress.

"Thank you," I told her. "You're a lifesaver."

"No problem." She smiled. "I might need you to get me out of an odd predicament one of these days."

"I doubt anything this weird would happen to you."

"You never know," she said. "You didn't put that dress on thinking you'd get stuck in it, did you?"

"Not in my wildest dreams," I said. "My client and I are very close in size, and I wanted to make sure the hem was hanging properly. She's picking the dress up this afternoon, and I need to finish it up. I figured I'd slip it on, see whether I needed to fix the hem, and then take it right back off."

Chuckling, Connie said, "Well, I'm glad I could help. I'd better get back to work. By the way, I have a sale on essential oils going on."

"I'll come over and check them out before I leave today," I said.

Connie left, and Max sidled up to me to sing, A Pretty Girl is Like a Melody.

As she sang, Zoe Flannagan came into Designs on You. Zoe, a high school student who was related to Max, could see and hear her. She began to dance with me to the song.

"What are you doing here in the middle of the day on a Friday?" I asked.

"We had early dismissal. Mom dropped me off. Can you take me home after work?"

"Sure."

"Cool." Zoe texted her mother to tell her she had a ride home. "What's been going on here today?"

"Our little Amanda got a dress stuck between her eyeballs and her thighs and had to run around like a flibberty jibbet until I texted Connie to come get her out of it," Max said.

Zoe laughed. "Are you serious?" She looked at me. "Is she serious?"

I nodded.

"A flibberty jibbet. That's a new one. Still, Aunt Max, you shouldn't use so many of your old flapper terms," Zoe said. "When I slip up and use one of them at school, everybody looks at me like I'm a total freak."

"Oh, ho, ho! Don't hang that hat on my coatrack, darling. I'll wager they thought you were screwy long before you met me." Max winked. "How's my precious nephew?"

Her smile fading, Zoe asked, "Could the three of us video chat with him later? He's bummed because one of his friends died."

"Aw, I'm sorry," I said.

"Of course," Max said.

Max's nephew, Dwight, was Zoe's grandfather. We found Zoe and Dwight several weeks ago when I was doing costuming for Winter Garden High School's production of Beauty and the Beast. Zoe was the stage manager. At the same time I was working on the play, Max asked me to try to discover what had become of her sister, Dorothy. I learned that Dot had given birth to two children—one of whom was a girl she named Maxine, after her sister. The other was a boy named Dwight.

Maxine had died young, but Dwight was living in a nursing home in Winter Garden. Like Zoe, he could see and hear Max. Other than me and Grandpa Dave—who also have a connection to Max—they're the only people we know of who can. So far, at least.

Zoe worked at the shop on Saturdays. I picked her up in the morning on my way to work, took her for food afterward—unless she and I decided to eat here and hang out with Max for a while first—and then drove her home. She often came by at other times during the week when she could get her mother to drive her. Her mom was a widower and worked two jobs. When Zoe couldn't be here, we often did video chats.

At the moment, she and Max were scrolling through Max's tablet to find something good to read. I'd opened up a whole new world to Max when I'd introduced her to electronic books, streaming shows, and social media.

After a perfunctory knock at the door, Ruby Mills entered the shop. Ruby had been one of my first clients—I'd made a dress for her granddaughter's wedding—and she'd quickly become one of my favorites.

I rose and gave her a brief hug. "Ruby, hi! How are you?"

"I'm well, but I need a knockout coat and hat. I thought I'd drop by here and see what you can fashion for me."

"Well, come on in and have a seat." After pulling one of the navy wingback chairs over for Ruby, I sat at the desk facing the door in the reception area. "Zoe, would you like to give us a hand?"

"Sure."

I introduced the two of them and explained to Ruby that Zoe helped out in the shop on occasion.

"I'd like to learn to make clothes like Amanda does," Zoe said.

"Well, you'll be learning from the best." Ruby smiled. "Are you two ready to design me something gorgeous?"

"Absolutely." I got my sketchbook and pencils. "What have you got in mind?"

"I want a white wool coat with a faux fur collar—also white. And a hat too. One of those like the gals in the 1920s wore."

"A cloche?" Max asked.

"A cloche?" I echoed.

"Probably. You'd know better than I would."

I searched for cloche hats on my laptop and then turned the screen around so Ruby could see the image results. "Is this what you're looking for?"

"Yes!" She clapped her hands together. "I want to look stunning when our church goes caroling."

"It's going to take a few days to make," I warned her. "When will you need it?"

"We're not going caroling until the night before Christmas Eve," Ruby said. "I have all the faith in the world in you."

When Ruby left, I blew out a breath. "I wish I had as much faith in my abilities as Ruby does."

"Zoe and I do," Max said. "And we'll help." She shrugged one slim shoulder. "Well, Zoe will. I'll supervise."

"That hat doesn't look like it would be all that hard to do." Zoe looked from the laptop screen to me. "Do you think I could make one?"

"I think you could." I leaned back in the chair. "I'll tell you what. I'll teach you how using Ruby's hat. Then, if you'd like to make some to sell in the shop, I'll give you the proceeds from them."

Her eyes lit up. "Really?"

"Really."

"That'd be awesome! When can we start?" she asked.

"As soon as I figure out how to make a cloche hat."

"It's almost closing time," Max said. "Do you think it would be all right if we call Dwight now?"

"Let's do it." I nodded at Zoe, and she opened a new tab on the laptop.

After logging into her social media, she called Dwight. "Hi, Papaw. Is this a good time for you to talk?"

Dwight shook his head. "No, honey, not right now. I'm about to lie down."

"What's wrong?" She sat up straighter. "Are you sick?"

"No. Not yet anyway." He sighed. "Another one of my friends died, Zo. I think these people are killing them. And I'm afraid I'll be next."

Chapter Two

Zoe said, "Papaw, we'll be there in a few minutes." She looked at me. "I mean, if Amanda can bring me."

Being tethered to Shops on Main, Max was unable to leave the building. Technically, she could go out onto the porches, but that was it. When I said her world really opened up thanks to social media, I meant it.

"I wish I could go too," Max said. "But this is good. Dwight and I can chat—just the two of us."

"If any of the nurses come in your room, Papaw, pretend you're not talking on your laptop, all right?" Zoe asked. She didn't want anyone to think he'd gone insane, since it would look as if he were sitting there talking to an empty room.

I put Jazzy in her carrier. It usually cheered Dwight to see the feisty feline.

On the drive to the Winter Garden nursing home, I asked Zoe, "Wonder why he's being so paranoid?" I'd only known Dwight for a few weeks and didn't know if paranoia was a part of his personality or if something had happened at the facility to make him afraid.

"I don't know," Zoe said. "He's had friends from there die before. It makes him sad, but he's never gone the I might be next route. That's pretty intense, in my opinion."

"Mine too."

Outside the entryway of the nursing home, I set down Jazzy's carrier. I was pretending to readjust my grip, but really, I was steeling myself for the smell. I'd recently heard on a podcast that the odor underlying the antiseptic smell in long-term care facilities wasn't urine, as was the common perception, but something called nonenal. Nonenal was produced when the skin generates more fatty acids and natural antioxidants deteriorate, thus leading to "old people" smell.

Picking up the carrier, I nodded at Zoe, and we went inside. We turned left and hurried down the hall to Dwight's room. He was sitting at the desk in front of his laptop and started when Zoe opened the door.

"It's all right, Papaw. It's just us."

"Dwight, I hope it's okay that Jazzy came to see you," I said.

"Oh, yes. I love Jazzy."

I pushed the door closed before letting Jazzy out of her carrier. She promptly crossed the room and hopped onto Dwight's lap.

"She adores you," Max said from the laptop on Dwight's desk.

"Did you ask if it's okay?" Dwight asked. "I'm trying to be really good."

"It's all right for Jazzy to be here." I had asked prior to bringing Jazzy on her first visit and was told it was fine as long as the cat didn't leave Dwight's room.

"Besides, you're always good," Zoe said. "You're better than good. Right, Aunt Max?"

"Absolutely!" She beamed. "Look what good stock he comes from!"

Apparently, Dwight didn't realize Max was a ghost. He had never questioned why she always wore the same clothes, and he'd never bothered to ask how she was Zoe's aunt. Given the fact that he was in his eighties and Max looked as if she were in her early thirties, it had probably never crossed his mind that Max was his aunt. All he seemed to care about was that Max looked like his mother and that they could talk through the computer. I guessed that was all he needed to know.

Grinning at Max, he said, "Still got all my hair and all my teeth."

"Me, too," she said.

"We're worried about you." Zoe sat on a nearby chair so she could look her grandfather in the eye.

"No need to worry about me, Dimples. As long as I don't step out of line, I'll be fine."

"What do you mean 'step out of line'?" I asked. "You aren't planning on robbing a bank or anything, are you?"

He chuckled. "No. I'd never do that. Can't run fast enough to get away anymore." His expression became grave, and he lowered his voice. "My friends were both known to raise a ruckus, and now they're dead."

Zoe stood. "I'm going to find out from the nurse what happened to them."

"You can't." His eyes widened. "You'll get me in trouble if you do."

"I agree," Max said. "If these palookas are knocking off troublemakers, the last thing we want to do is make healDwight out to be one."

Patting Dwight's thin shoulder as he continued to stroke Jazzy's head, I said, "What if we offer to send flowers to your friends' families? That's not troublemaking—that's being considerate."

"All right. I suppose that would be okay—as long as you don't raise a ruckus."

I lifted my right hand. "I solemnly promise no ruckus-raising. Be right back."

At the nurse's station, I found one harried-looking nurse with her dark hair in a severe bun. "Yeah?"

"Hi. I'm Amanda Tucker, and I'm here with Zoe Flannagan."

"Dwight's grandkid, yeah. What do you need?"

"Well, two of his friends from here died, and he's pretty distraught," I said.

"Right. Bea and Mack." She picked up a pen. "I'll give Dwight something to help him sleep."

"Oh, no, no." I held up a hand. "Thank you, but that isn't necessary. I don't think he'll have any trouble sleeping. He just wants to send some flowers to the funeral home for the families."

"Huh." She seemed surprised. Apparently, nursing home patients weren't in the habit of sending flowers to the funeral homes for their friends. "That's not necessary—the nursing home sends an arrangement."

I smiled. "He's old fashioned. Brought up by a Southern mom who always sent flowers and took food when a friend passed."

"Weren't we all?" She barked out a laugh. "Well, if he really wants to send flowers, he can send them to the families of Bea Jansen and John McCready at Peaceful Rest Funeral Home over near Brea Ridge."

"Thank you."

"I don't mind giving Dwight something to calm him and make him sleep," she said.

"I appreciate that. We'll let you know if he needs it."

When I returned to Dwight's room, he and Zoe were playing checkers while Max coached them both from the laptop. Dwight was happily winning, and Zoe was teasing that he was too tricky.

I sat on the windowsill where Jazzy had moved to and was looking out onto the parking lot. I rubbed her chin as I watched the checkers match progress.

Within a few minutes, the nurse I'd spoken with gave a brief knock before coming into the room. Dwight froze, his red checker in mid-air. If the nurse wondered why the interior of a fashion boutique was up on Dwight's laptop, she didn't mention it. I wasn't near enough to close it. Not that the nurse could see Max, but I simply didn't want Dwight to be questioned about what he'd been doing after we'd gone.

"Visiting hours are almost over, folks," the nurse said.

Max poked her tongue out at the woman.

"We doing okay here?" She squinted at Dwight. "Need any help going to sleep tonight?"

"No, ma'am." He put the checker on the board.

"I'll be at the desk until midnight if you should need anything." She turned her attention back to me. "Ten minutes."

"All right. Thank you," I said.

Zoe and Dwight finished their game, and then Zoe put away the checkers as I secured Jazzy in her carrier.

"Love you, Papaw." Zoe kissed his cheek. "We'll see you soon."

"Love you, Dimples." He looked around the room. "You, too, Amanda, Jazzy, and Aunt Max."

"We love you," Max said. "Don't you worry about a thing. You're going to be fine."

Dwight nodded but didn't look convinced.

"Are you two coming back to the shop?" Max asked me.

"I think we'd better get something to eat and then get Zoe home," I said. "I'll try to touch base with you a little later."

"All right. Ta!"

I couldn't always reach Max. It took a lot of energy for her to stay present at Shops on Main as much as she did.

When we got back into the car, Zoe asked, "So, what do you think?"

"I've got a bad feeling." I backed out of the parking space. "For one thing, that nurse was awfully eager to give Dwight something to make him sleep. She asked me twice and him once if he needed medication. What do you think?"

"I've never known Papaw to spook easily, and his friends' deaths have him on edge," she said. "Is there someone we could call or something we could do?"

"Yeah. We need to find out what killed Bea and Mack," I said.

Zoe grasped my arm. "Do you think it could be an overdose of sleeping pills?"

"I don't know." Surely, the nurse wouldn't be that bold. Would she? "Either way, I feel it warrants some looking into. First things first—let's call Grandpa Dave and see if we can drop in at his house."

Chapter Three

Grandpa Dave, Zoe, and I sat at his dining room table with takeout boxes in the middle of the table. We had paper plates and cups, so clean up would be a breeze later. My laptop showed Max sitting at my desk at Designs on You. We wanted her to be included in our conversation.

Jazzy was eating her food at her bowls in the kitchen. We visited Grandpa Dave so often that he had food and water bowls as well as a supply of her favorite food on hand.

"So, tell me what's got my favorite ladies concerned," Grandpa Dave said.

The three of us started talking at once, so he asked us to let Zoe begin.

"Papaw is really scared, Dave. Two of his friends are dead, and he thinks that if he doesn't be good—that's exactly how he worded it—he'll be next."

"I went out to the nurse's station and asked the nurse there the names of Dwight's friends," I said. "I thought I could use their names to find out what had happened to them."

"You didn't ask the nurse their causes of death?" Grandpa Dave asked.

"No, I didn't feel it was appropriate, and I didn't want to make waves for Dwight. I told her Dwight wanted to send flowers." I took a sip of my soda. "The thing that concerned me about the nurse was how willing she was to give Dwight a sleeping pill."

"Not only did she ask Amanda at the desk, she came to the room and asked again," Max said. "She wanted to knock my sweet nephew out."

"Let's not rush to judgment, dear." Grandpa Dave smiled. "I love how protective all of you are, but we need to find out everything we can about Dwight's friends so we can give him some reassurance."

"True." Zoe got out her phone. "The nurse said they were at Peaceful Rest, right?"

"Yes. And their names were Bea Jansen and John McCready," I said.

Zoe tapped some keys while Grandpa Dave and I ate, and Max looked at her fingernails.

"No cause of death is listed for either," Zoe said at last. "Bea's obituary says she went to be with her Lord and Savior, and Mack's simply says he passed away. From there, it gives us visitation and funeral information. That's it."

I hadn't expected the cause of death to be listed in the obituary. Had there been a request for donations to cancer research or something of that nature, we might've inferred a cause of death. But neither obituary requested charitable donations.

"When is the visitation?" Grandpa Dave asked.

"Bea's family is receiving guests tomorrow evening, and the visitation for Mack will be on Sunday." Zoe frowned slightly. "I don't know if I'll be able to go to either one without my mom freaking out."

Zoe's mom, Maggie, was one tough customer, but she loved her daughter. Having never been inside Shops on Main, Maggie's ability to see Max had never been tested. Max and I had asked Zoe if she'd like to invite her mom inside, but she'd told us Maggie wasn't open-minded when it came to ghosts. Seeing a ghost—even a family member as awesome as Max—would terrify her, and Zoe was afraid Maggie might make her quit her job at Designs on You if she believed there was anything other-worldly going on there.

"Has Dwight ever mentioned Aunt Max to your mom?" Grandpa Dave asked. "I'm guessing that would freak her out."

"Oh, it definitely would," Zoe said. "I told him when we first started talking with Aunt Max that it would be best if we didn't tell Mom about our video chats—that they would be our fun little secret." She smiled. "When I was in elementary school, our fun little secret was that Papaw would always sneak me candy. But he'd make me promise to eat all my dinner so Mom wouldn't find out and make him stop spoiling me."

"As much as I'd like to meet your mom, I'm thrilled to have you and Dwight in my life," Max said. "Of course, I was thrilled with Amanda and Dave too! My family just keeps growing!"

"I wonder if Dot spoiled her children," I said.

"I'd imagine she did." Max laughed. "Dottie always loved to bake, and she'd make me treats whenever I was feeling down."

"I can't imagine you ever being down." I shook my head in disbelief. "You're always such a positive person."

"Of course, I am now, darling. I'm dead. What have I got to lose?"

I didn't have a response to that.

"Papaw told me lots of stories about how Great-Grandma Dot would surprise him with a cake or a pie whenever he did well in school or earned some accomplishment. And sometimes they were flat-out bribes."

"Like what?" Max rested her chin on her fist. "Tell me about one of the bribes."

"One time, she wanted Papaw to ask a girl in his class to the sock-hop." Zoe held up her hands. "Now, according to Papaw, this poor girl was as ugly as a mud fence, but he agreed to ask the girl because Great-Grandma Dot had promised him an entire coconut cake all to himself if he would. She apparently felt sorry for the girl."

"Of course, he asked her," I said.

Grandpa Dave chuckled. "And I'm guessing that girl blossomed into a beauty and became your grandmother."

"The girl did blossom but ended up married to the richest boy in town. Papaw said he used to brag that he'd seen a diamond beneath that lump of coal all along. Then he met Mamaw and shut up about the coconut cake girl."

After sharing in the hearty laughter, I got up to take the trash into the kitchen.

"Let me give you a hand with that," Grandpa Dave said. "Zoe, hon, keep Max company, will you?"

Once we were in the kitchen, he lowered his voice. "Between you and me, did you think Dwight was overreacting about his friends' deaths?"

"I don't know the man very well, but I find it hard to believe he'd be as frightened as he appeared to be this evening without good reason—at least, in his mind." I tossed the empty plates into the garbage can. "But also the nurse's eagerness to sedate Dwight made me think she could be in the habit of controlling any unruly patients through medication."

"If this woman is using sedatives to control her patients' behavior, Dwight could see their health failing, contribute it to their being anesthetized, and believe she'd killed them."

I shrugged. "Maybe, in that way, she did."

Zoe came into the kitchen carrying my laptop. "Max said to tell you guys goodnight. She needs to restore her energy."

"That sounds like a good plan for all of us," I said. "I'd better get you home."

"I'll put Jazzy in her carrier," she said. "Thanks for being the host with the most and the ghost, Dave."

"You're welcome, sweetie."

I kissed Grandpa Dave's cheek. "I'll give you a call tomorrow. Would you mind going to Bea Jansen's visitation with me?"

"Not at all," he said. "We need to offer Dwight some reassurance."

Jason called when I was driving home from dropping off Zoe.

"Hello, beautiful. I've just finished up with a client who wants me to shoot his daughter's winter formal," he said. "I'm guessing it's too late for this evening, but are you free for dinner tomorrow night?"

"I think so." I'd have to work dinner with Jason around Bea Jansen's visitation. "Even though I've already had dinner with Zoe and Grandpa Dave, would you and Rascal like to come by and watch a movie with Jazzy and me?"

Zoe and I had planned to stream The Bishop's Wife tonight—Max, too, if she could maintain enough energy—so we could all discuss it at work tomorrow.

"Sure," Jason said. "I'll swing through a drive-through and get something to eat, and Rascal and I will be there in an hour or so."

"That sounds great," I said. "It'll give me time to make some movie snacks."

"So, what are we watching?" Jason asked when he and his wild white dog entered my living room an hour later.

I didn't answer right away, as Rascal had scampered over to me and was entreating me to scratch his furry head. Laughing at the way Rascal wiggled his entire body as he danced around me, I answered, "The Bishop's Wife."

"I've never heard of it. Is it new?"

"Hardly. The film was made in 1947."

He scrunched up his face. "Is it sappy?"

"Maybe a little, but you'll love it."

"I do appreciate the nuances of black and white cinematography." He kissed me. "I'm glad it's Friday."

"Me, too." It had been a crazy week, and Jason and I hadn't seen each other very often despite working in the same building.

We sat on the sofa, and I turned on the television.

"Before we watch the movie," I said, "do you know anything about the nursing home in Winter Garden?"

"No. Why?"

I explained about Dwight and how he'd acted so odd that Zoe and I went over there to check on him. "He's afraid the nursing home people are going to kill him."

"That's extreme, don't you think?" He shook his head. "Does he have dementia? I know people with dementia can get paranoid."

"I don't think he does. Grandpa Dave and I are going to the funeral home tomorrow to see what we can learn about Bea Jansen, one of Dwight's friends who died." I shrugged slightly. "We thought if we could find out the cause of death, then we could reassure Dwight."

"If you can provide Dwight reassurance and he is still afraid of the nursing home staff, then you might suggest to Maggie that he needs a psychiatrist or a neurologist."

"But, Jason, what if he's right?" I asked.

"You've been watching too many crime shows. But, if it'll make you feel better, I'll ask my friend Ryan—he's a deputy at the Winter Garden Sheriff's Department—to see if he can get a cause of death on Dwight's two friends."

I smiled. "Thank you."

"You're welcome." He kissed me again. "Now, let's watch this sappy Christmas movie."

Chapter Four

Jazzy was dozing on the backseat in her carrier as we drove from Zoe's house to Shops on Main.

"I tried to call Papaw before I left the house, but he didn't answer," Zoe said. "He's probably still sleeping."

"Is that normal for him?"

"Yes." Her voice betrayed her anxiety. "Why? Are you worried maybe that nurse came back and gave him a sleeping pill after we left?"

"No." In truth, I was a little. "We can go by and check on him before I take you home after work, if you want."

"We'll do that if I can't get him on video chat before then."

Ella and Frank were in the hallway when we arrived at Shops on Main.

"Good morning, ladies," Frank said. "We're on our way for coffee. For some reason, it's always a little tougher for me to wake myself up on a Saturday."

"It's because when you worked at the manufacturing plant, you always slept in on Saturdays," Ella said.

"Ah, yes, before I retired. Now I live this life of luxury." He rolled his eyes at us comically.

Zoe giggled. "Well, I'm glad you're here and not there, Frank. Had you not been here, who'd have helped Amanda make the ottoman costume for *Beauty and the Beast*?"

She had a point. Frank had been instrumental in making that costume for the play.

"We're glad *you're* here," Ella told Zoe. "Having you around the building for the past few weeks has made me miss our grandchildren like crazy. Our son's family lives near Boone, so Frank and I don't get to see them as often as we'd like." She stepped into the kitchen and poured her coffee. "Thank goodness, the kids will be here to spend a few days with Frank and me soon."

Ella headed back to Everything Paper, and Frank got his coffee.

Watching his wife's retreating back, he said quietly, "We see those kids plenty. They're little monsters. Their mother browbeats our poor Oliver half to death, and the kids have her crummy disposition."

"Frank, did you get lost?" Ella called.

"Coming!" He gave us another eye roll before hurrying off down the hall.

Zoe grinned. "We need to help Frank find a project to do while the grandkids are in town."

"I'll see if Grandpa Dave has any suggestions." I opened the door to Designs on You and placed Jazzy's carrier on the floor. When I let her out, the cat immediately rushed over to Max.

Max was perched on the worktable, but she appeared more translucent than normal.

Hurrying over to her, Zoe asked, "Are you all right?"

"No, darling, I'm dead." Max winked. "You know that."

"That's not what I meant." Zoe huffed.

Laughing, Max said, "I know. I'm fine, as far as I know. I just haven't got a lot of energy today. Still, I wanted to pop in and discuss the movie."

I wasn't as concerned as Zoe because I'd seen Max with her energy depleted before. She'd rest up for a day and be back to herself the next time we saw her. "Did you love it?"

"I did." She fanned herself with both hands. "Cary Grant—what a dreamboat!"

Zoe looked from Max to me before visibly relaxing. "Queenie, the dog, was like Jazzy. She could see the angel even when he was invisible to everyone else."

"That dog was sweet," I said. "Jason watched the movie with me. He said had he been the bishop, he'd have punched Dudley."

"Did you point out to him that the bishop wouldn't have been justified in attacking a man for wanting something he himself seemed determined to push away?" Max asked.

"I said something to that effect."

"And what did he say?" Zoe poured some dry food and water into Jazzy's bowls.

"He said, 'you're telling me that if I don't treat you well, you'll run off with an angel?' Of course, I said I would."

"My mom thought I was nuts because I cried when Dudley left," Zoe said.

"Why would she think that?" I slid Jazzy's carrier under the worktable. "It was sad."

"Yeah, but movies seldom make me cry." Zoe turned away and busied herself with straightening bolts of fabric on the shelf. "But it made me think of you, Aunt Max. Will Amanda and I come in one day, and you—you'll be gone?"

"I don't know, darling." Max moved closer. "I don't know why I'm here or how long I'll stay; but since I've been here for—what? Eighty years?—I doubt I'll be ankling out of here anytime soon."

Before Max could say anything further, Trish Oakes, the building manager, came into the shop.

Max gave Zoe and me a wave before fading out of the room.

"When Mrs. Meacham was overseeing the management of Shops on Main, she made it a practice to have the shopkeepers draw names for a Secret Santa Christmas gift exchange," Ms. Oakes said. "Would you like to be a part of this tradition? There's a twenty-dollar spending limit, and gifts will be exchanged next Sunday."

"Sure. That sounds like fun." Glad she gave us plenty of time to find something for our recipient.

Ms. Oakes held out a basket filled with strips of paper. She had apparently anticipated everyone would take part in Secret Santa.

I was desperately hoping I'd get Connie's name as I drew a slip of paper from the basket. I opened the slip of paper and tried not to show my dismay as I read *Trish Oakes*.

"You didn't draw yourself, did you?" she asked.

"Nope." I plastered on a smile.

"Have a pleasant day, Amanda." Ms. Oakes left.

"Who'd you get?" Zoe asked.

I handed her the slip of paper.

She grimaced. "Dang—that's the worst person you could've gotten."

"You're telling me."

Zoe and I searched online until we found a downloadable cloche hat pattern at an Etsy shop called Elsewhen Millinery. I didn't have a printer in my shop, so I left Zoe in charge and went upstairs to borrow Jason's.

The door to his studio was open. I always left the doors to Designs on You closed to keep Jazzy inside.

Jason was sitting at his desk painstakingly retouching a family photo.

"Nice looking family," I said, kissing his temple.

"Thanks." He smiled. "This is a welcome surprise. I need a break."

"Would you mind opening another tab on your computer so I can print out a hat pattern?"

"No problem." He opened the tab and then got up, giving me his chair.

I sat and logged into my email account. "Are you having a good day?"

"I am. Retouches are always a little tedious, but they make the photos look so much better." He stretched his arms up over his head, and his shirt rode up slightly to show his toned midriff.

Finding the email from the Etsy shop, I downloaded and printed the pdf pattern. "I have a client who wants a cloche hat, and Zoe had the idea of making some for the shop. I told her she can keep the profits from her sales—I'm guessing she can use the money."

"You're really good for her," Jason said.

"She's good for me. It's great to have some help in the shop, even if it is only one day a week."

"Whose name did you get for that Secret Santa thing?"

"We're not supposed to tell," I teased. "That's why it's called secret Santa." I lowered my voice. "But I got Ms. Oakes."

"Yikes. What are you gonna get the old dragon?"

"I have no idea. Who'd you get?"

"Can't tell you—it's a secret." He grinned.

I arched a brow. "I told you."

"All right. I got Frank."

"Lucky! Frank will be easy to buy for."

"Oh, really? Then tell me what to get him," he said.

"I will, if you'll tell me what to get Ms. Oakes."

"Sorry, beautiful—you're on your own." He gave me a quick kiss. "I have to get to an appointment. May I escort you back down the stairs?"

"Of course." I nearly shuddered at the remembrance that Max had died falling down those very stairs.

When I returned to the shop, I told Zoe, "Jason got Frank."

"Would Jason be willing to swap with you? Frank would be a breeze to buy for. I think he'd like about anything you'd get him."

"Right?" I shook my head. "But, no, Jason won't swap. I do have our pattern, though. And, thank goodness, I have enough white wool on hand to make both Ruby's hat and her coat." I went to the shelf and took out a bolt of red wool. "I thought you could make your first hat at the same time I'm making Ruby's. I've always found it easier to learn by doing."

Since it was an even busier Saturday than usual given that it was prime holiday shopping season, we only managed to get the hats cut out. Still, it was a start.

"Did you ever reach Dwight?" I asked Zoe, as we put the pattern pieces aside to sew up on Monday.

"Yeah, and he's fine."

"Would you still like to go see him today?"

"No," she said. "I believe he'll be okay until Mom and I visit him tomorrow."

"All right. If you change your mind, let me know."

"I'm kinda concerned because we haven't seen Max in a while." She looked around the room, obviously hoping our friend would appear.

"I doubt we'll see her again today," I said. "She needs to recuperate from being present for so long yesterday."

"Are you sure?" she asked.

"I'm positive." I didn't tell Zoe, but since she'd mentioned it this morning, I'd also begun to wonder if one day we'd come into the shop and Max would be gone— just like Dudley the angel in *The Bishop's Wife*.

Chapter Five

I stopped and got Zoe a pizza on the way to her house. She could have a slice or two for lunch, and then she and her mom could heat up the rest for dinner. That way, Maggie wouldn't have to cook when she got home from work.

When I got to my house, I changed into comfy sweats before going online and placing an order with my favorite fabric wholesaler for a few bolts of wool in various colors. I wanted Zoe to have a variety of colors on hand for her hats, but I knew that going into winter I'd need more wool as well—especially when Ruby showed off her new coat while caroling.

After ordering the fabric, I spent a relaxing afternoon in the living room near the Christmas tree. I read while Jazzy snoozed on my lap.

As shadows lengthened in the room, I turned on the tree lights. I'd decorated it much as my mother had every other year. Habit, I guess—or tradition. I often felt conflicted that everything in the house was mine but not. You see, this had been my parents' home before they'd moved to Florida. The only rooms I'd redecorated after they left were my bedroom and the guestroom, which I turned into a sewing room.

Looking at the tree made me feel nostalgic. I considered calling Mom, but I changed my mind. She and Dad were planning on coming to visit in a few weeks. I'd talk with her then.

Mom and I had a strained relationship. She didn't believe I was living up to my potential and thought I relied too heavily on her father-in-law, Grandpa Dave. Dad and Grandpa Dave shared a lot of the same personality traits, and he and I got along great. We had such a strong rapport that I thought Mom sometimes got jealous of our relationship.

I glanced at the clock and saw that I needed to get ready to meet Grandpa Dave at Peaceful Rest.

I wore a navy, 1940s-style victory suit to the funeral home. Grandpa Dave was already there waiting for me at the door.

"Hi, Pup." He kissed my cheek. "How was your day?"

"It was great. Yours?"

He opened the door for us. "The casserole crusades have begun."

"Oh, no." I hid a smile. "I'm sorry."

The casserole crusades had gone on every year around the holidays since Grandma Jody had died. Various women brought casseroles to Grandpa's house hoping they might set themselves up with a beau for the coming winter. Not that I could blame them—who wouldn't want a handsome older guy squiring them around to church, Bingo, and the occasional grandchild's birthday party?

"How was Dwight today?" he asked.

"He seemed to be in better spirits when Zoe spoke with him this afternoon."

A funeral home director approached and softly asked, "Which family are you here to visit this evening?"

"Jansen," I said.

"The Jansen family is in the room to the far right," he said.

Having serious misgivings about coming to pay my respects with regard to someone I didn't even know, I took Grandpa's arm.

He patted my hand. "It's all right," he whispered. "I've done this far too many times to count."

We signed the condolence book before getting in line behind the other visitors. I heard people speaking in hushed tones about Bea:

"She went downhill so quickly. She seemed fine in October, and here only a few weeks later, she's gone."

"She didn't seem at all like herself the last time I saw her. She was so subdued."

"Laurel thought maybe she was depressed."

"I believe she was—had to be. She had such a sharp wit—"

"—strong opinions about everything—"

"—and she became so listless—"

"No spark whatsoever. She seemed tired all the time."

Grandpa Dave and I exchanged knowing looks. I could tell we were both thinking about Dwight's assertion that he was "being good" so he wouldn't be next.

At last, we got up to the casket. I was relieved it was closed. I didn't know whether I'd ever seen Bea Jansen at the nursing home, but I knew I didn't want to see her this evening.

"Laurel Sanders," a small, soft-spoken woman said, extending her hand. "How did you know my mother?"

"We didn't," I said, enveloping her hand and giving it a brief shake. "I'm Amanda Tucker, and this is my grandfather, Dave. Our friend, Dwight, was close to your mom, and he wanted us to come on his behalf."

"Dwight." Ms. Sanders smiled. "Yes. They used to have fun together."

"I know he misses her terribly," Grandpa said.

"I understand Ms. Jansen wasn't afraid to raise a ruckus," I said with a grin.

"Oh, no, she sure wasn't." A cloud seemed to move over Ms. Sanders' face. "At least, she wasn't until recently. She wasn't herself at the end. It was as if she simply got tired of living and gave up."

"We're very sorry for your loss." Grandpa patted Ms. Sanders' shoulder. "If you should need anything, please let us know."

With a hand on my back, he guided me through the room and back to the lobby of the funeral home.

"Are you thinking what I'm thinking?" I murmured.

"Yeah. Dwight might be on to something."

I turned my head sharply to look up at him.

"I'm not saying he's exactly right," he said, "but I wouldn't be surprised to learn that Bea was being sedated."

"Me either. Want to ride to the McCready visitation together tomorrow?"

He nodded. "I'll pick you up."

When I got home, I changed my skirt for a pair of jeans to dress down my outfit for my date with Jason. Then I fed Jazzy and gave her fresh water.

By then, Jason was knocking on the door.

I greeted him with a kiss. "What do you have in mind for tonight?"

"I have a surprise for you."

His words made me nervous. Although I smiled and didn't say anything, I wondered, *What kind of surprise? He's not taking me to meet his parents, is he? I didn't know whether or not we were that far along in our relationship; but even if we were, I didn't want that meeting to be a surprise.*

As we drove to our surprise destination, Jason asked, "Did you and Dave go to Bea Jansen's visitation?"

"We did. It was sad. Her daughter—and other people standing around us—spoke about how she'd gone from being lively to being subdued," I said. "Her daughter thinks she lost the will to live."

"That's possible, you know."

"I know. But given what Dwight said…"

He nodded. "I spoke with Ryan—the deputy I know in Winter Garden—today. Turns out, Dwight is a cousin or something. Anyway, Bea Jansen and John McCready's official causes of death was heart failure."

"Did you say anything to Ryan about Dwight's suspicions?"

"I did. He didn't seem terribly concerned about it, but he told me to let him know if there were any further developments."

"Further developments." I turned the words over in my head. "Meaning what? Let him know if they start doping up Dwight?"

"I believe he meant if we saw any suspicious behavior."

"Oh."

We pulled into the Brea Ridge Carriage Company.

Turning to Jason with a widening smile, I asked, "Are we—?"

"Yep. A carriage ride to see the Christmas lights followed by hot cocoa and cookies by the fireplace in the reception area."

Chapter Six

I was still waking up—Jazzy hadn't even stirred yet—when my phone rang. My heart started racing as I grabbed the phone from the nightstand and fumbled it onto the bed before getting it into close enough proximity to answer the call. The phone indicated the call originated from an unknown number—hospital? Fire department? Police? The possibilities flooded my befuddled brain as I answered.

"Hello?"

"Amanda? I didn't wake you, did I?" The man's voice was vaguely familiar.

"Who's this?"

"Oh, sorry. It's Ford. You know, from Antiquated Editions."

"Ford, what's wrong?"

"Nothing's wrong. Take a breath." He chuckled. "Shucks, I did wake you up, didn't I?"

"No. I'm just not used to getting calls from unfamiliar numbers so early on a Sunday morning," I said. "I thought there had to be something wrong."

"Nope. Everything's fine." He paused momentarily. "I am in a little bit of a pickle, though, and I—well, *Connie* and I...that's who gave me your number—thought maybe you could help."

"Does this pickle involve alterations?" I didn't know of any other dilemma Ford might have that I could be of any assistance with.

He gave another laugh, and this one sounded even more forced than the first one had. "Actually, my niece is going to be spending a few days with me."

"That's nice." I still didn't see what that had to do with me or why the situation had prompted Ford to call me at seven o'clock on a Sunday morning.

"Um...yeah...Sienna is a fantastic kid. Her mom has a new job and can't take any vacation time yet," he said. "So, since Sienna's school has already closed for winter break, I'll be bringing her to work with me for a few days."

I was beginning to see where this was going, but I didn't say anything.

"Connie said she'll be glad to help me keep the munchkin entertained," Ford continued, "since I'm guessing she'll get bored with my dusty old books quickly. And Connie mentioned that Sienna and Zoe might enjoy hanging out together."

"That's true, but Zoe only works on Saturdays." I didn't want to be rude to Ford or his niece, but I felt it was pretty presumptuous of him if he planned to pawn his babysitting duty off on Connie and me.

"Won't she be there more when school is out?" he asked.

"Not unless her mom can drop her off," I said. "She doesn't drive yet. I go pick her up on Saturdays, but I can't do that every day. Besides, Winter Garden is still in school for at least part of this coming week."

"Oh." He was quiet for a moment, and I knew he was coming up with another angle. "Still, I'm sure Sienna would enjoy seeing the fascinating work you do. I'll bring her down and introduce her to everyone tomorrow morning."

"Okay." I felt as if I should say I'd look forward to it, but I simply couldn't bring myself to form the words. While I wouldn't mind meeting the child and maybe even taking her to lunch a time or two, I had too much work to do to give up hours of my day. And then there was Max to think about...

"Oh, hey, while I have your ear, what's something Connie might like?" Ford asked. "I drew her name in that Secret Santa thing."

"I imagine Connie would like almost anything you'd get her," I said. "A pretty scarf, a tree ornament, a pair of gloves…" I was planning on giving her a pretty mug and some chocolates.

"Yeah, any of those would work. Thanks," he said. "By the way, who'd you get?"

"Ms. Oakes."

"Ugh. Hate that for you. I'd get her a gift card to—to somewhere nice."

"That would feel as if I didn't put any thought into her gift whatsoever," I said. "Do you know of *anything* she might like?"

He was quiet for a moment, so I figured he was thinking over my question. At last, he said, "Sorry, kiddo. I've got nothing."

Maybe Max could help.

Once I'd finished talking with Ford, I opened the social media app on my phone to see if Max was active online. She was. I sent her a video chat request.

Accepting, she smiled at me and said, "Well, look who rises with the sun—even on the weekend."

"Do I look bright-eyed and/or bushy-tailed to you?" I asked.

"Sure, chickadee. You seem all right to me. But I'm guessing you're not."

I told her about Ford's call.

"Yikes," she said. "I don't want some little crumb-snatcher cramping our style."

"Neither do I. But how can I politely extricate myself from doing Ford's babysitting for him?"

"That's easy, darling. You say *no*." She propped herself up on my chair, shook her hair, and said, "Try me—ask me anything."

"All right." I affected a *Ford* voice. "Max, this is Niece. She's ever so interested in sewing. Can you show her the ropes?"

In a tone as sweet as sugar, she replied, "No. I'm far too busy. Maybe I can work with her for a few minutes at the end of the day. I'll come up and get her."

I sat up straighter. "Hey, that was good—you didn't sound mean at all."

"It wasn't mean. It was honest. Why didn't modern women ever give up the notion that to be nice one has to be a doormat?"

"I don't know," I said. "I guess it was passed down from one generation to the next that 'good girls' are helpful and go out of their way to be kind."

"Then I say poo on being a good girl." She winked. "Santa isn't watching. And even if he is, he'll put Ford on the naughty list for planning to take advantage of you and Connie."

"Speaking of Santa, after you left today, Trish Oakes came around and had us draw names for Secret Santa." I grimaced. "I got her."

"Her? The old wet blanket herself?"

I nodded. "What should I get her?"

"A personality."

"There's a twenty-dollar limit," I said.

"Applesauce. In my day, you could've maybe got her a sense of humor or some compassion with twenty clams, but I realize a greenback doesn't stretch as far as it used to."

"Have you ever heard Ms. Oakes mention something she likes? Or overheard her listening to music?"

"No, but I don't go around her if I can help it. She's too negative," she said. "Want me to check out her office and look for clues?"

"Would you mind?"

"Nah. It'll be as easy as passing through a wall." She ginned. "That's about as much as I plan to exert myself today. I'd hoped to talk with you and maybe with Dwight." Her smile faded. "Did you and Dave learn anything at the funeral home?"

"Lots of people were talking about how Bea was only a shell of the woman she'd been in the weeks before her death." Jazzy came over and butted her head against my chin. "Whether that was due to natural causes or sedation, I can't say."

Max took a moment to speak to Jazzy before asking me Bea Jansen's cause of death.

"Heart failure," I said.

"What do you plan on saying to Zoe and Dwight?"

"You know Zoe always has her internal lie detector on—I have to shoot straight with her."

"And Dwight?" she prompted.

"At this point, we know nothing for certain. I feel we need to reassure him rather than alarm him."

She nodded. "That's fine, darling, as long as we also protect him."

Chapter Seven

Following my chat with Max, I got up, showered, dressed, put Jazzy in her carrier, and headed to Grandpa Dave's house. The air was colder this morning, so I was glad to see Grandpa had turned on the gas logs in the fireplace. I was even happier to find that he'd made breakfast.

"Good morning, Pup." He kissed my cheek before taking Jazzy's carrier. "Come with me, Ms. Jasmine. I believe you'll be delighted with what you find in your dish."

He took the carrier to the kitchen and opened the door. Jazzy didn't even take time to make her usual swish around his ankles—she darted straight to her food bowl where tuna, cheese, and diced hard-boiled egg awaited her.

Seeing the chafing dishes on the sideboard filled with bacon, hash brown casserole, and scrambled eggs, I felt as excited as Jazzy. "What's the special occasion?"

"Aw, I got to missing your grandmother last night, that's all." He gave me a sad little smile. "Remember how she used to make all those wonderful breakfasts for us on the weekends?"

"I do. I always thought the Queen of England couldn't possibly eat any better than we did when Grandma Jodie made a special breakfast." Grandma had been an excellent cook in other respects, but she outshone herself with breakfast. I snagged a biscuit from the breadbasket and bit into it. "You've done her proud."

"Thanks. But you can get a plate, you know."

"Really? I thought I'd just eat out of the pans." I got a plate and some silverware, and Grandpa did likewise. "How are the two of us going to eat all this? Or are you expecting company?"

"No, it's just us," he said. "I wish Zoe could be here. I feel like she'd enjoy a hearty breakfast."

"I think you're right." I filled my plate.

"Have you spoken with your mom or dad?"

"Not in the past week," I said. "I guess I should give them a call."

"You should." His tone was light and not at all admonishing, even though I knew he wished I'd get in touch with my parents more often. "They've decided to postpone their visit until January."

Putting my plate down on the table, I turned to look at Grandpa Dave. "What? They aren't coming home for Christmas?"

He shook his head. "Too much traffic this time of year, the plane tickets are at their highest rates during the holidays, they want to visit when they'll have more time to spend here—yadda, yadda."

"But we've never missed Christmas with Mom and Dad." I tried to keep the whine out of my voice. I wasn't sure I succeeded.

"I know, Pup. But this way, we'll get to celebrate twice."

Leave it to Grandpa to find the silver lining.

He poured us both a cup of coffee. "I'd like to invite Zoe and Maggie to spend Christmas Eve with us, if you don't think they have other plans or that asking them over would be too presumptuous."

"I believe it's a wonderful gesture. I'll run it by Zoe before we mention it to her mom," I said. "I'd also like for the three of us to do something special for Max."

"Of course, we will. I imagine she has years of missed celebrations to make up for."

"Yeah. Even if she observed other people's festivities, she didn't get to join in. How awful would that be?"

"Don't be sad," he said. "We just said we're going to make this year fun for her."

"I know. I'm not sad...although I am kinda bummed that Dad and Mom won't be here for Christmas, though. Aren't you?"

He shrugged. "We always knew they'd leave the nest and start their own traditions one of these days. I guess we'll have to make the best of it."

"I suppose we will," I said. "Inconsiderate so-and-sos." Zoe wasn't the only one adopting some of Max's vocabulary.

After breakfast, Grandpa and I had sung Christmas carols as we cleaned up the kitchen. Now, as we drove toward Brea Ridge, I could feel my cheerful mood fading.

"I really hope we find that John McCready was as irascible as ever when he died of something other than heart failure," I said.

"So do I." Grandpa pulled into a parking space at Peaceful Rest. "But even if he was as mellow as a lamb and had a coronary, it doesn't mean the nursing home folks did anything untoward. Old people's hearts give out."

"I know. It would be an odd coincidence, though, the two of them, same symptoms, same cause of death within hours of each other."

When we stepped onto the porch, a white-haired gentleman opened the door for us. "Peter Finlay." He extended a hand to Grandpa.

"Dave and Amanda Tucker," Grandpa said, shaking the man's hand. "We're here for the family of John McCready."

"Of course. I'm the director here at Peaceful Rest, and I wanted to say it's nice to see you again so soon."

Peter Finlay didn't really appear to believe it was all that nice to see us. It was more like he thought our being at his funeral parlor two days in a row was suspicious.

"Bea Jansen and John McCready were both friends of Dwight Hall," I said. "We're here on his behalf."

"And is Mr. Hall a resident of Winter Garden Nursing Home?" Mr. Finlay asked.

"He is."

"We provide services to a lot of people from the nursing home, but other than the occasional nurse, no one from the facility—and certainly none of the other patients—tend to visit to pay their respects." He folded his hands. "I find it refreshing that you not only sent flowers to the family but are attending services on Mr. Hall's behalf."

"How did Mac die?" Grandpa asked.

"Heart failure," Mr. Finlay said.

"Is that a common occurrence among nursing home patients?" I asked. "I believe Bea Jansen also had heart failure."

Mr. Finlay nodded gravely. "Yes. Poor dears. Sometimes their tickers simply stop ticking."

"Have any of Mac's family members mentioned that he wasn't himself lately? We heard several people at Bea's service saying that about her, so we were curious." Grandpa's face was as impassive as if he were asking about the weather.

The funeral home director wasn't fooled. "Why, whatever do you mean? Do you think there's some sort of virus spreading through Winter Garden Nursing Home? Or are you concerned the patients aren't being properly cared for?"

"Oh, no, we—" I began.

"I'm on the Board of Directors at Winter Garden Nursing Home," Mr. Finlay interrupted. "And I can assure you nothing untoward is happening. Winter Garden patients get the best of care."

"We know they do," I said, quickly backtracking because I was terrified of making trouble for Dwight. "One of the reasons Dwight was so upset about his friends' passing was because they hadn't been active in the days leading up to their deaths. While we feel sure that's because their health was declining, he thought maybe he'd hurt their feelings."

Mr. Finlay raised his folded hands to his chest. "Ah, our long-term care residents are so like children sometimes, are they not? Please reassure Mr. Hall that his friends still cared about him and that their health was merely diminished."

"We'll do that," Grandpa said. "Nice chatting with you."

As we walked toward the room where John McCready's family was receiving guests, I looked back around at Mr. Finlay. He was scowling. Catching my eye, he quickly contorted his face into a benevolent smile. I wasn't buying it.

After Grandpa and I had given our condolences to John McCready's family, we went back out to the car.

"I think we rattled Mr. Finlay's cage," I told Grandpa. "Do you think we should go to the nursing home and check on Dwight?"

"I do," he said. "And I think you should call Jason when you get home and ask him if his friend Ryan learned anything interesting about the recent deaths there. Mr. Finlay can say what he wants, but unless someone comes down with a serious illness, I find it hard to believe their personality would completely change in the days prior to their death."

"Not to the extent those people were talking about. I heard someone whisper that Mac had gone from a curmudgeon to a zombie within a week." I buckled my seatbelt. "Barring a brain injury or trauma, I can only chalk that level of change up to sedation."

Chapter Eight

I had called Jason on my way home from Grandpa Dave's, and he'd invited me to come over and watch a football game on TV with him and Rascal. So, I'd gotten Jazzy settled in, grabbed a box of dog treats and a bag of potato chips, and I drove to Jason's apartment building.

It was drizzling when I got there, but luckily, I found a parking spot near his place. Spaces were limited, and they were often full.

Jason's apartment was on the lower level, and he met me at the door with a blanket. Draping the blanket over my shoulders, he said, "That rain is cold."

I laughed. "Thank you. You're pretty thoughtful, you know."

He nodded at the chips and dog treats. "So are you."

Rascal tried to wedge himself between us, and Jason took the chips, treats, and my purse so I could pet the dog.

After slipping off my jacket and hanging it on the back of one of the bistro chairs in Jason's kitchen/dining room combo, I went over into the living room to look at his tree.

"I haven't been here since you put your tree up," I said. "This is really pretty."

The tree was over six feet tall and stood in front of the living room window. It boasted an ornate star topper, and blue and silver ornaments. A complementary ribbon garland was wound around the tree from the top to the bottom. I was impressed. My tree wasn't anywhere close to being this coordinated.

"That's my mom's handiwork." Jason came to stand beside me. "She put it up yesterday while I was working."

"It's beautiful."

"Yeah…Mom likes match-y stuff." He scrunched up his face. "It's gonna be a pain in the butt to take it all down and store it."

"Maybe you could put it in the corner of your home studio-slash-office," I said. "That way, you could do Christmas photos any time of the year and just move the tree back to the living room when next Christmas rolls around."

He pointed his index finger at me. "That's not a bad idea."

Nodding toward the TV, I asked, "What's the score?"

"Still nothing to nothing," he said. "You haven't missed anything."

Even if the score was twenty-four to three, I wouldn't have thought I'd missed anything. I didn't even know who was playing. "I'm going to put the chips in a bowl. Want anything else while I'm scrounging around your kitchen?"

"Nope. I'm good."

Jason's kitchen was tiny. Maybe *compact* was a better word. The carpeted dining room was merely an extension of the living room. The linoleum divided the dining room from the kitchen. On the right was the washer and dryer, and the refrigerator was on the left. There was plenty of cabinet space, an oven, and a dishwasher. He even had a garbage disposal—I kinda envied him that because I didn't have one.

The kitchen was an efficient use of space, but I imagined only one person could cook in it at a time. We'd never put my theory to the test. When we ate at Jason's— and often, at my house—we had takeout.

I put the chips into a bowl, tucked Rascal's treat box under my arm, and returned to the living room. Jason was already sprawled onto the large blue sofa.

Rascal danced around my feet until I sat down beside Jason.

I handed the chips to Jason and opened Rascal's box. As I fed treats to the dog, Jason asked me how the funeral home visit went.

"It went," I said. "The funeral director was a little creepy. He wondered why Grandpa and I were there two days in a row."

He chuckled. "Did you tell him you just really enjoy the ambience at Peaceful Rest?"

"No. We explained that both Ms. Jansen and Mr. McCready were Dwight's friends and that we were there on his behalf."

"And did Mr. McCready also die of heart failure?" he asked.

"Yeah. Plus, we overheard people in the receiving line talking about how Mac had gone from curmudgeon to zombie in less than a week." I fed Rascal another treat before he climbed onto my lap. "The funeral director told us he's on the board of directors of Peaceful Rest. I got a bad vibe from that man."

"Would you like me to call Ryan?"

I nodded. "If you don't mind. You did say you'd already spoken with him and that he's looking into the deaths, right?"

"Yep." He muted the television and made the call. "He'll come by in just a few minutes."

I was nervous about meeting one of Winter Garden's finest, but Deputy Ryan Hall wasn't as intimidating as the detectives I'd previously met. In fact, he was rather attractive—not as handsome as Jason, but cute, especially in his brown uniform.

Ryan moved Jason's recliner slightly to face the sofa to make it easier to talk with us. On Jason's command, Rascal lay down. Jason gave him a stuffed toy to chew on, and the dog was content. He seemed to realize Ryan was here to discuss something serious.

"Is it all right for you to be here?" Jason asked. "Aren't we out of your jurisdiction?"

"A little." He shrugged. "But Winter Garden Nursing Home isn't, and the dispatcher will call if I'm needed elsewhere. So, Amanda, tell me what you've observed."

I told him about Dwight and how he seemed to think that if he was bad, he'd die like his friends did. And I explained about the nurse being very willing to sedate him. "We could all be overreacting, but I have a really bad feeling."

Ryan's lips twitched. "My girlfriend, Amy, gets *bad feelings* too. And she's usually right. Besides, Dwight is somehow related to me on my Dad's side of the family, so I can't ignore the situation."

"Did you learn anything about any of the other recent deaths?" Jason asked.

"There's a lot of heart failures." Ryan spread his hands. "The coronaries could be brought on by over sedation; but if it's being done only by one nurse who is sedating residents to make them submissive during her shift, they'd likely be all right at other times of the day."

"Unless the entire nursing staff is involved in keeping problem patients sedated," I said.

"Right." Ryan stood. "I'll keep digging. In the meantime, keep an eye on Dwight."

"We will." I stood too. "Thank you for looking into this. If nothing else, we can hopefully put Dwight's mind at ease."

"I hope it's nothing," Ryan said. "But the bad news is that autopsies are rarely performed in nursing home settings, so misconduct is hard to prove. Again, be vigilant."

Jason walked Ryan to the door. When he returned, I was looking at my phone.

"What is it?" he asked.

"Ryan's right." I nodded at my screen. "This news article says that in a wrongful death suit where an elderly man's death was ruled as *natural causes*, his demise was found to have been actually brought on by poor care. He had infected ulcers, was dehydrated, and had pneumonia."

He got out his phone and searched the internet to see what he could find as well. "Listen to this case: Investigators determined Ms. Poole's death was hastened by unnecessary doses of antipsychotic drugs, which may have lethal side effects for seniors."

"Was this Ms. Poole in a nursing home too?" I asked.

Jason nodded.

"But antipsychotic drugs require a prescription, right? How was she being given the medication without a doctor's consent?"

"The doctor was the one who was being investigated for misconduct in Ms. Poole's case," he said.

As we sat on the sofa, we forgot all about the football game and learned some more disturbing facts. According to one news article, we learned that doctors often err regarding cause of death in elderly patients. The piece cited a study in which nearly half the doctors surveyed failed to correctly identify that an elderly patient had died from a brain injury caused by a fall. One reporter concluded that medically reasonable assumptions and bias were responsible for the lack of investigation into nursing home patients' deaths.

At last, I snuggled up under the blanket and nestled against Jason's side. Rascal dozed at Jason's feet as the football players battled on the TV screen. I wished I could be a fly on the wall and know how Dwight was being treated. And then it dawned on me—I couldn't, but maybe Max could.

Chapter Nine

I went in to work early on Monday morning hoping to talk with Max before Ford and his niece arrived. After unlocking the door to Designs on You and letting Jazzy out of her carrier, I gave her some kibble and water before going into the kitchen and making a pot of coffee.

"You know, I always thought coffee smelled better than it tasted," Max said, materializing by the refrigerator. "But I imagine it's tastier now than it was in my day. We didn't have all the flavored blends and creamers that are popular now. Mother's java was as dark and thick as motor oil."

"I wish you could have a cup to see for yourself." Knowing I might be interrupted soon, I said, "I'm really glad you're here, though."

"It's unusual for you to be here this early, so I figured there was something on your mind."

I quickly told her about the funeral home visits, the meeting with Deputy Hall, and what Jason and I had read online. "I found myself wishing I could be a fly on the wall in Dwight's room. That way, I'd know what was going on when the staff thought Dwight was the only one there."

"I wish there was some way *I* could be that fly," Max said.

"I believe you can."

She squinted. "You know I'm tethered here, darling."

"Not to the extent you used to be."

Max caught on quickly. "I see where you're going, but I don't understand how I can be at the nursing home virtually without the staff thinking my poor nephew is bananas."

"If you aren't visible, Dwight won't even be aware you're there," I said. "I was hoping maybe Zoe could leave her muted phone in his room for a full day."

"Would that work?" Max asked. "Even if we could have me be there virtually, would Zoe be willing to give up her phone? She's positively glued to that thing."

"I'll try to talk with her when she gets out of school today." The coffee finished brewing, and I poured myself a cup. "I considered a nanny cam, but—"

"A what?" Max interrupted.

"A small, hidden camera to record what happens when someone is away. The term was coined because parents use them to ensure their children are being properly cared for by the babysitter when they're away." I stirred cream and sugar into my coffee.

"Wow." She shook her head. "What a sad commentary on the world. But why did you decide the hidden camera wouldn't work?"

"It *would*, and we might resort to it yet," I said. "But if something happened and you were virtually there, you could let me know and I could immediately put a stop to it." I heard Ford's truck pull into the lot and sighed. "You know how I hate confrontation."

"I know, darling. But chin up! I'm going to stay and walk you through this."

"Good morning!" Ford's voice boomed through the hallway.

"Hey, Ford," I responded. "There's fresh coffee."

"Fantastic." He came into the kitchen. Trailing in his wake was a sullen little girl of about nine or ten years old. "Sienna, say hello to Amanda."

"Hi." Sienna crossed her arms over her chest.

"Hi, Sienna," I said. "It's nice to meet you. Are you looking forward to spending time with your Uncle Ford this week?"

"No. This place is boring." The child heaved a dramatic sigh.

"Amanda has a cat," Ford said.

Max gave a cry of indignation. "Don't sic the child on our precious Jasmine!"

"So?" Sienna scowled at Ford. "I don't like cats—they're mean."

"Since when?" he asked.

"Since my friend April's cat scratched me."

"Give that child a job," Max said.

"What kind of job?" I asked. Naturally, my words made Ford and Sienna look at me like I was crazy. I cleared my throat. "What kind of job would you like to have when you're older, Sienna?"

"I'm going to be a spy...or a detective. I read spy and detective books all the time, so I'm already pretty good at it." She jutted out her chin as if daring me to contradict her.

"Perfect." Max clasped her hands together. "Have her find out what to get Ms. Snooty Britches for Secret Santa."

"That's a great idea!" You'd think I'd have learned by now not to respond to Max when we were in the presence of others, but it was a reflexive response. "You could be a spy for me! I can pay you."

Sienna's eyes brightened and she unfolded her arms. "How much?"

"Does five dollars a day sound fair?" I asked. "Plus, I'll buy you a notebook and colored pens from Everything Paper to keep your observations in."

Ford frowned. "Amanda, what are you talking about?"

"I'm offering your niece a job to find out what I can get Ms. Oakes for a Secret Santa gift," I said.

"Hey, that *is* a great idea." He poured his coffee. "I need a little spying done myself."

"Fine. I'll work for both of you. But, Uncle Ford, you'll need to pay me seven dollars a day instead of five because you didn't offer to buy me a notebook and pens."

"I think I like this kid," Max said.

"Would you do it for five a day and a book from my shop?" he asked.

"Maybe. You got any detective books?"

Ford couldn't quite hide his smile. "We'll have to go see."

"As soon as I put my coat and things away upstairs, I'll be down to get the details of my assignment," Sienna told me. "Are you okay with me working for Uncle Ford at the same time I'm on your clock?"

"Sure. As long as you get the job done, your time is your own."

She thrust out her small hand. "I'll do my best for you."

I shook her hand. "I have the utmost confidence in your abilities."

When Sienna turned and started down the hall toward the staircase, Ford gave me a look of astonishment and mouthed, *How'd you do that?*

I smiled and shrugged.

When Max and I were back in Designs on You and I'd heard Ford and Sienna clomping up the stairs, I said, "You're an absolute genius, Max. How'd you know giving her a job would work?"

"Darling, I don't care how old a person is—or isn't— she wants to feel valued. Giving her a job gives her something to keep her occupied during the day while she's stuck here with her uncle, and the pay provides a reward she can happily anticipate." She perched on the worktable beside Jazzy. "Having her spy on Oakes was inspired, though. What a gasser!"

"Thanks, but I'd have never even considered giving her a job if you hadn't suggested it." I laughed. "I was able to avoid an awkward conversation, and I might gain some insights into what makes Trish Oakes tick."

Within minutes, Sienna the Spy came knocking. "I'm ready." She came inside and closed the door. "I read the note."

I had notes on both entrances to Designs on You requesting visitors to keep the doors shut so Jazzy couldn't get out. I doubted the cat would have much interest in wandering around Shops on Main—especially since Max spent her time here with us—but I couldn't risk her getting outside and into the busy highway.

"Where is your cat?" Sienna asked.

Jazzy was still sitting on the worktable with Max.

I nodded in their direction and asked, "Would you like to pet her?"

"No, thank you. Not until I'm sure she won't bite or scratch me." She rubbed her nose. "Everything Paper is open now."

"Then let's go introduce you to Frank and Ella and get your supplies."

"I'll pop back in later," Max said.

I waved goodbye.

"Do you always wave to your cat?" Sienna asked.

The tinkling of Max's laughter reverberated in her wake.

"Fairly often," I said.

Frank and Ella were still hanging up their coats when Sienna and I went into the shop.

"Good morning. This is Sienna, Ford's niece."

"It's a pleasure to meet you," Frank said. "I'm Frank, and this lovely lady is my wife, Ella."

"Hi." Sienna was already looking at notebooks. "I'm in a hurry because I need to get to work."

Frank grinned. "Ford has your nose to the grindstone already?"

"I don't know what that means, but I am working for Uncle Ford and for Amanda." She put her notebook and pens on the counter.

"What sort of work do you do?" Ella asked.

"I have a fledgling detective agency. They want me to find out what they should get for their Secret Santa people."

Ella raised her brows. "What's your going rate?"

Max popped back in as I was cutting out Ruby's coat. "That's going to be gorgeous."

"Thanks. Where's our little spy?"

"She's in Trish Oakes' office."

"Already?" I laughed. "I'm impressed."

"So am I. The kid's got moxie."

"Does she ever. We went to buy the notebook and pens, and now she's working for Frank and Ella too," I said. "I think maybe one of them got my name because they scheduled their meeting with Sienna after lunch—of course, lunch is included in their payment."

"I love it! That's the elephant's eyebrows."

Jazzy yawned, stretched, and got out of her bed to come see Max.

"Hello, lovely," Max said. To me, she asked, "Would you like to know which one of the Petermans drew your name?"

"No." I waffled. "Yes." I waffled again. "No."

"Which is it, Toots?"

"No." I bit my lip. "No. It's supposed to be a surprise."

"All right. *Frankly*, I'd want to know. I hate to be kept in suspense."

"So, it's Frank."

She pursed her lips. "I didn't say that."

My cell phone rang. I frowned when I saw the caller identification—it was Zoe. She shouldn't be calling this time of day when school was still in session.

"Hey, Zoe. Is everything okay?"

"No. I spoke with Papaw before school this morning. Another one of his friends died last night."

Chapter Ten

After calling Grandpa Dave and asking him to meet me at the nursing home, I put a note on the doors saying I'd gone to lunch and headed toward Winter Garden. Max promised to stay with Jazzy. Although Max couldn't physically restrain Jazzy if the cat started to get into something toxic, she could move. That's all Max ever had to do—wherever she went, Jazzy followed. Not that there was anything particularly dangerous to Jazzy in the shop—no poinsettias and only one small artificial tree on the mantle, keeping the picture window free for displaying clothes. Jazzy had never been a cord-chewer, but it was always best to err on the side of caution; and I felt better knowing Max was there with her.

These were the banalities I flooded my brain with to avoid wondering what I might find when I reached the nursing home. Mainly, I was afraid Dwight might be heavily sedated by the time I got there. If he was upset before Zoe left for school, had he been able to hide his agitation from the nurse with the penchant for administering sleeping pills?

Grandpa Dave was already there when I arrived. He was waiting for me in his truck. Luckily, there was an empty parking space beside him. I pulled in, parked, and locked the car. Grandpa motioned for me to get into the truck.

I opened the door and hopped up onto the passenger seat. "Thank you for coming. I hope this isn't disrupting your day."

"Not at all, Pup. Glad I can help. But after all your sleuthing over the weekend, what do you think is going on here?"

"Honestly, it could be nothing more than our buying into Dwight's fears," I said. "I do know the one nurse I spoke with on Friday was more than willing to give him a sleeping pill he didn't need. But who knows? Even that could've been regulation—I'm sure nursing home staffers want to keep their residents calm and happy."

"And sedated patients are calmer," Grandpa said. "Yet that solution should be the exception rather than the rule."

I told Grandpa about some of the horror stories Jason and I had found online.

"Just because you read a news article or two about some isolated cases doesn't mean anything untoward is happening here." He opened his door. "Now, let's go make sure it isn't."

We went inside, signed the visitors' log, and hurried to Dwight's room. He was sleeping.

"Should we wake him?" I asked.

"I don't know. Let's ring for a nurse." He pressed the nurse call button on the bedrail.

A voice came over the intercom. "Yes, Mr. Hall?"

"Could I see you please?" Grandpa asked.

There was an audible sigh before the voice responded, "I'll be there momentarily."

Within two minutes, a chipper woman with a warm smile strolled into Dwight's room. "Hi, there." Her eyes darted from Dwight's sleeping form to Grandpa and me. "Did he fall asleep that quickly?"

"He was sleeping when we got here," Grandpa said. "I'm the one who rang for you."

"You certainly seem more cheerful now than you did over the intercom," I said.

The woman chuckled. "That wasn't me. You spoke with Penelope—I'm Sally Jane."

I noticed Sally Jane wore jeans and a sweater rather than scrubs or a nurse's uniform. "Are you off-duty? We don't want to bother you if you aren't on the clock."

"No, honey, I'm a volunteer. I come here on Mondays, Wednesdays, and Saturdays to help out."

"That's awfully thoughtful of you," Grandpa said. "Do you have family here?"

"No, but that's all right." She gave another throaty chuckle. "I feel like I get back more than I give."

Jerking my head toward the bed, I asked if there was somewhere we could talk where we wouldn't disturb Dwight.

"Sure. Let's go to the cafeteria."

Grandpa and I followed Sally Jane down the hall and into the lunchroom where many residents sat with their trays of food. It appeared they were having chicken, mashed potatoes, and peas today. As we passed the tables, Sally Jane spoke to many of the diners, calling them by name. They seemed to adore her.

We made our way to a small corner table.

"I can get y'all a plate if you're hungry," Sally Jane said, pulling out a chair and sitting where she could keep an eye on the residents.

Grandpa and I thanked her but declined the offer.

I searched his eyes seeking some sort of reassurance. He knew me so well that he gave me a brief nod letting me know that he, too, trusted Sally Jane.

"Sally Jane, is Dwight feeling well today?" I asked.

"He was upset when I first got here this morning," she said. "One of his friends died up in the night. I know the staff tries to keep residents from knowing right away when someone passes, but they always know."

"Did one of the nurses give him a sleeping pill?" Grandpa asked.

"Maybe. They do that sometimes—it's common. In Dwight's case, if they did, I think it was a good idea. It was apparent to me that he'd been awake most of the night. It was almost as if he felt afraid to go to sleep." She picked a napkin up off the table and began tearing it into tiny scraps. "I feel sorry for these sweet souls, living here in this place...knowing they'll never—well, you know."

"You told us you thought in Dwight's case it would have been a good idea for him to have been given a sedative today, if he was given one," I said. "Do you ever feel the staff doles out sleeping pills unnecessarily?"

Sally Jane's sharp eyes looked from me to Grandpa before scanning the room. When she spoke, her voice was just above a whisper. "I don't want any trouble."

"We don't either." I gave her an abbreviated version of Dwight's behavior since Friday. "We're not sure if Dwight is simply being paranoid or if he's right to be concerned."

She bit her lip. "He's correct in assuming that if he gets too rowdy or contentious, he'll be given a sedative.

But I don't believe anyone would purposefully harm him." Scanning the room again, she added, "That said, I do believe some of the nurses are too quick on the draw when it comes to sedation."

"The resident who died last night," Grandpa said, "was the cause of death heart failure?"

Shaking her head, she answered, "He fell and hit his head."

"That's terrible." I decided to go ahead and ask the question I'd been dancing around. "Sally Jane, do you think there are any shady practices going on here?"

"I don't know. That's a question I've been asking myself lately, and I don't have an answer." She looked down at the tiny pieces of paper now scattered on the table like the world's most boring confetti. "I'm not even sure I want an answer. If I know there's something hokey going on around here, then I'll have to try to fix it. And I don't have a clue about how to do that."

"We'll help you," Grandpa said.

She swept the paper off the table and put it into a nearby trash receptacle. "Let me think on it. I don't want to get kicked out of here. This isn't my job, so I wouldn't suffer any financial loss; but I love these people, and they love me. I'm the only person some of them have to visit with."

"We understand," I said. "And we'd never do anything to jeopardize your position here. But we know that—like us—you have the residents' best interest at heart. All we want is to make sure they're being properly cared for." I took a business card from my purse. "Please give me a call anytime."

Grandpa Dave and I left then. When we were outside, he asked if I'd like to go to lunch.

"I'd love to, but I'd better get back to the shop and start sewing Ruby Mills' coat up."

"All right, Pup. I'll talk with you in a bit."

On the drive back to Shops on Main, I called and left Zoe a message: "Grandpa Dave and I went to check on your papaw—he's doing fine. Talk with you after school."

I didn't tell her he was sleeping because he'd likely been given a sedative. I knew that information would make her worry herself sick—which was the last thing she needed on a day when she was taking mid-term exams. I felt confident Sally Jane would check on Dwight another time or two before she left, and I could go see him again after work.

I really hoped to hear from Sally Jane soon. It would be great to have more inside information about Winter Garden Nursing Home.

Chapter Eleven

Max was anxiously awaiting my report when I returned to Designs on You.

"We might have someone on the inside." I told her about Sally Jane. "Her heart is in the right place, so I'm hoping she'll agree to help us."

"What shape was my nephew in when you got to the nursing home?"

"He was asleep." I raised a hand before Max could interrupt me. "I asked Sally Jane if she thought he'd been sedated. She said maybe and admitted it was a common practice, but she said it was apparent Dwight had been awake most of the night." I gulped. "She got the feeling he'd been afraid to go to sleep."

Max closed her eyes and lowered her head.

"Either way, I believe the rest will do him good," I said. "And Sally Jane will look out for him while she's there today. Even if she ultimately decides not to help us, I'm confident she'll make sure he's being treated properly while she's in the building."

"Who was the friend who died?" Max asked.

"His name was Clarence Perkins. He didn't die from heart failure but from a blow to the head he suffered during a fall."

"Oh, my goodness." Max paced. "This is disastrous. We have to get Dwight out of that horrible place."

"If it isn't safe for him to be there, we will," I assured her.

"It's *not* safe. I just know it's not."

I wished I could give Max a hug or a reassuring pat on the shoulder. "Why don't you rest for a little bit, so you'll have plenty of energy when we call Zoe after school?"

"That's not a bad idea. I'll see you soon." With that, Max was gone.

I picked up my phone to call Jason, but there was a sharp knock at my workroom door. I was crossing the room to see who was there when Jason poked his handsome head inside.

"Hello, beautiful." He came on into the room, closed the door behind him, and gave me a quick kiss. "How are you?"

"Better now. As a matter of fact, I was getting ready to call you." I smiled. "You must be psychic."

"Actually, Dave called. He's bringing us a large calzone from Milano's for lunch." He nodded toward the worktable. "If you'll clear us off a spot, I'll get some drinks from the fridge. Dave should be here any minute."

I quickly moved the cut-out pieces of Ruby Mills' white coat and hat to the shelf on the other side of the room to avoid getting any grease or marinara sauce on the fabric.

Jason came back with the soft drinks and several paper towels to spread onto the area where we'd be eating. "It's nice of Dave to do this."

"It is. He's one in a million."

Grandpa arrived then with our delicious-smelling lunch. "Hi there."

"Hey, Grandpa. You didn't have to do this," I said.

"I know, but I had a hankering for one of these calzones and knew I couldn't possibly eat the whole thing myself."

"You could if you didn't get one as big as half outdoors." I kissed his cheek before I went to the kitchen and got us each a plate and a set of utensils.

"I'm glad you got a big one," Jason was saying when I returned. "I'm hungry."

"So am I, and I believe Amanda is too." Grandpa opened the box and took the plastic knife I handed him. "She took her lunch break visiting the nursing home."

"Did something else happen?" Jason asked. "Is Dwight okay?"

"He's fine," I said, "but another of his friends died—this time from injuries sustained in a fall."

"We do think Dwight might have been sedated." Grandpa cut the large calzone into three pieces.

Jason looked at me. "Have you spoken with Ryan?"

"Not yet. I thought I'd try to reach him sometime this afternoon." I cut the portion of the calzone Grandpa had given me in half and returned part of it to the box. "I *am* hungry but not famished." I laughed. "*Your* eyes always have been bigger than *my* belly."

"Just want to be sure you always have enough, Pup." He looked down at Jazzy who'd gotten out of her bed to sit by his feet. "You, too, Jazzy—we'd never let you go hungry."

We chatted about mundane things while we ate. I knew Grandpa was probably wondering where Max was, and I hoped I'd get the chance to tell him before he left. If not, I'd give him a call.

Sienna joined us just as we'd finished eating. "Hey." She addressed the group in general.

"Hi, Sienna. This is my grandpa, Dave. And have you met Jason already?"

"No. We haven't met, but I know he's the photographer who has the place next to Uncle Ford's." She nodded. "Nice to meet you both."

"Sienna is not only Ford's niece, but I've hired her to be my spy. I need her to help me figure out what to get Ms. Oakes for her Secret Santa gift."

"Uncle Ford and Mr. and Mrs. Peterman hired me to do some work for them too," Sienna said. "Do either of you need a detective?"

"I'm in good shape at the moment," Grandpa said, "but I'll keep you in mind. Have you got a business card?"

"Not yet, but I'll have some tomorrow." Sienna looked at Jason. "How about you?"

"I don't want you to get overworked your first day here," he said. "But see if you can work me into your schedule mid-week."

She nodded. "You got it." Looking at me, she asked, "Would you like a preliminary report, or would you prefer to wait until I have the whole thing?"

"Go ahead and give me a preliminary report please. That way, if I have any follow-up questions, you can take care of them." I gestured toward the piece of calzone in the box. "Are you hungry?"

"No, thank you. I just got back from lunch with the Petermans. It looks good, though. May I take it to Uncle Ford?"

"Sure," I said.

"Mom calls him a garbage disposal." She shrugged. "She said he always was one."

"Do you have any brothers or sisters, Sienna?" Grandpa asked.

"No. I think I might like to have one someday. It might be fun to have a business partner."

I suppressed a smile. Sienna had been in business for less than a day and was already seeing the need to take on a partner. Granted, she *did* have the business of half the merchants in the building.

"Now about Ms. Oakes." She glanced toward Grandpa and Jason before turning her attention back to me. "Is it all right to speak freely in front of these two?"

"You may," I said.

She flipped open her notebook. "I told Ms. Oakes I wanted to talk with her about running a business. She invited me into her office to chat. There was a skinny Christmas tree in the corner of her office decorated with purple and silver ornaments. She had a stack of books on the corner of her desk with sunny covers."

"Sunny?" I frowned.

"Yeah, you know, like at the beach," she said. "I told her the books look nice, and she said she loves the beach. That's all I have so far."

"Excellent work." I smiled. "Thanks."

"I'll have my full report and invoice for you by the end of the day." She closed the box and plucked it off the table. "Thank you for this pizza thing."

"You're welcome," I said. "I hope Ford enjoys it."

"He will."

Jason got up and opened the door for her. After she went through, he closed it back and said, "That one's a force of nature, that's for sure."

"She's got some gumption all right," Grandpa said.

"Who'd have thought Trish Oakes loved the beach so much?" I stacked up the plates and gathered the utensils.

"And that was your *preliminary* report." Jason resumed his role as doorman, so I could take our trash to the kitchen.

I came back, closed the door, and sat back down at the worktable. "Back to what we were talking about earlier—do you think we should call the deputy?"

"It's whatever you want to do," Jason said.

"Would you be providing him any pertinent new information?" Grandpa asked. "Yes, there was another death, but this one wasn't like the others. I feel you'd be better served if you could provide Deputy Hall with some hard evidence the next time you contact him—give the man something to work with."

"That's an excellent point, Dave."

I held up my crossed fingers. "Fingers crossed that Sally Jane will give us the help we need."

Gayle Leeson

Chapter Twelve

I was applying interfacing to pieces of Ruby's coat when Max reappeared that afternoon.

"Hi, there," I said. "You look as if you feel better."

"I do." She smiled. "I've gone decades without being a worrier. Then you people come along and, suddenly, I'm pacing the floor."

"Sorry." I put my work aside and moved into the reception area to log onto social medial from my laptop. "Let's see if Zoe is home from school yet."

Seeing that both Zoe and Grandpa Dave were currently online, I sent video chat requests to them. When they accepted, I could see Zoe in her bedroom with a print of

Edgar Allan Poe behind her; and there was Grandpa sitting in his living room.

"Where's our sassy specter?" Grandpa asked.

"I'm here, silver fox." Max sat on the desk so she could be visible onscreen.

"Hi." Zoe stifled a yawn.

"Are we boring you already, darling?" Max asked.

"No. I stayed up late last night studying for today's exam," Zoe said. "Amanda, thanks for your message. I didn't have time to respond because I was taking my test."

"I assumed as much," I said. "I just wanted you to know your papaw was fine."

"He was sleeping when we got there," Grandpa said, "but we don't know if it was because he was exhausted or because the nurse had given him a sleeping pill."

"Either way, Sally Jane seemed to think he needed the rest." I quickly explained who Sally Jane was and that, hopefully, she was going to help us discover what—if any—shady practices were going on at the nursing home.

"Pup, after I got home today, I was thinking about the person who died last night—Clarence Perkins. The name sounded so familiar, but I couldn't figure out why. I asked around and found out Clarence was the brother of one of my casserole crusaders."

"What in the world is a casserole crusader?" Max asked.

"It's a woman who's trying to woo Grandpa Dave before winter sets in, so she brings him casseroles," I said. "The casserole crusades have occurred around this time every year since Grandma Jodie died."

"Are the casseroles good?" Zoe asked.

"Some are, but my freezer is getting full," Grandpa said. "You think you and your mom might like one or two?"

"Sure." Zoe grinned. "I might even let Mom think I cooked."

"So, did your casserole crusader give you any information on Clarence?" I asked.

"Yeah. She told me Clarence was a diabetic." He pushed his glasses up on his nose, indicating we were about to get a lecture. "The nursing home's policy is that all unused prescription medications are returned to the dispensing pharmacy for disposal when a patient dies. Clarence's daughter is a registered nurse, so she asked for a list of the medications returned to the pharmacy so she could make sure her dad had been receiving the proper dosages. She, too, was concerned by the number of recent deaths at the nursing home."

"Did they give her the list?" I asked.

"They did, but there was no insulin on it," Grandpa said.

Max gasped. "He was a diabetic with no insulin? How did they explain that?"

"They couldn't." He lifted his shoulders. "The staff member the daughter spoke with has no idea what happened to the rest of his insulin. She thought maybe it had just ran out on the day he died."

"That would be convenient," Zoe observed.

I rubbed my face. "Does this nurse believe her dad wasn't getting his insulin?"

"She doesn't know. My friend said the daughter wanted an autopsy but couldn't afford to have it done." Grandpa removed his glasses and cleaned them on his shirttail.

"If the nurse wants an autopsy, why can't she get one?" Zoe asked. "Doesn't the nursing home or the insurance company pay for that?"

Putting his glasses back on, Grandpa said, "Nope. The doctor already signed off on Clarence's cause of death, and he saw no need for an autopsy. The family would have to pay for a private autopsy in this case, and they run between three and five thousand dollars."

"Yikes." Zoe scrunched up her face. "That doesn't seem fair when she's not sure her dad was getting his medication."

"Zoe, I wondered if you'd care to leave your phone in your papaw's room one night so Max can hang around and see what might be happening there when no visitors are around," I said.

Her brow furrowed. "Yeah, I should be able to make that work."

There was a problem with her leaving her phone—I could tell. "Are you afraid to leave your phone because your mom would be concerned?" I asked.

"If she missed it, she'd have a fit," Zoe said. "And I'm on my phone a lot, so she'd notice if I wasn't texting or anything all night. But I want to make sure Papaw is safe."

"Don't you think we might ought to tell Maggie that we're concerned about what's going on at the nursing home?" Grandpa asked.

Zoe took a deep breath. "Not yet. She'd probably think Papaw and I both were overreacting."

A striking woman in a beige silk suit and a royal blue coat walked into the reception room.

"Hi," I said. "Welcome to Designs on You. Let me put this laptop in my workroom, and I'll be right with you."

"We can hang up and resume the call when you're finished with your customer if that would work better," Max said.

Smiling and avoiding the temptation to respond to Max, I took the computer into the workroom, placed it on the table, and closed the door behind me before returning to the reception area.

"Thank you for your patience," I told the woman. "Are you looking for anything in particular today?"

"As a matter of fact, I am." She sat on one of the blue wingback chairs near the window. "I want a dress—something like they'd wear on *Downton Abbey*...the upstairs people."

I chuckled. "Gotcha. I'll grab some pattern books, we can see what styles appeal to you, and then I can make you a custom dress that would do Lady Mary proud."

"Will it be expensive?" she asked.

"Yes."

She gave a succinct nod. "Good. Will everyone *know* it's expensive?"

"Well, you can tell everyone it's a custom design," I said.

"I could do that with any old off-the-rack dress."

"You could." I inclined my head. "But if you buy from me, you won't have to worry about someone else showing up in the same dress."

"Let's get started then." She gave me a wry smile. "I feel the need to explain so you won't think I'm a total snob."

"You don't have to explain anything to me," I told her.

"Well, I want to. My husband's company is having a *Downton Abbey* themed Christmas party. All the women there act as if I'm second class, and I want to show them that I'm not."

I got up and retrieved the pattern books. "You don't need to prove anything to anyone. I was impressed with you the moment you walked in. But if you feel the need to show off, I've got you covered." It was hard to believe that a woman this elegant and outwardly self-assured was actually insecure.

We were able to find a pattern we liked for a sheath dress with an embroidered overlay and a sash. I grabbed my sketchpad. Giggling like two schoolgirls, we created a beautiful maroon gown with a gold overskirt.

"Do you have a tiara? If not, we'll have to get you one," I said.

"I will." She laughed. "I didn't dream this would be so fun. What's next?"

"I'll get some measurements, and then I'll make a muslin pattern for you. Once that's done, I'll give you a call and have you come in for your first fitting. In the meantime, I'll order your fabric so that after we make sure the muslin pattern fits properly, I can make the actual dress." I grabbed my gold pencil and made her some gloves. "Gold opera-length gloves are a definite must as well. Want me to order them?"

"Absolutely!"

Sienna came through from the workroom then. "Hi. Why is your grandpa and some girl talking to each other on your computer?"

"Um...I need to take care of that." I hurried into the workroom. "Sorry, guys, I'll have to give you a call back, all right?"

"Sure, Pup," Grandpa said. "Talk to you soon."

By the time I returned to the reception area to reclaim my client, Sienna was explaining to her that she was a detective who'd been hired to learn about some of the people who work here.

I told Sienna I'd check with her later and that I needed to take some measurements from my client. She said okay but handed me a folder before she left. I was guessing her report and invoice were inside it. Having her around was going to make it an interesting week.

My client—who I'd discovered was Marsha Billings—came through to the workroom. "She's a little firecracker, isn't she?"

"You wouldn't believe."

Chapter Thirteen

After Marsha Billings left, I clipped together the patterns I'd use to make her dress, and then I ordered the materials I'd need. Having done all I could do for my new client at that point, I picked up the file Sienna had marked TOP SECRET. Grinning, I opened the folder to find a neatly printed report and some illustrations.

The report reiterated what Sienna had already told me about Ms. Oakes' skinny Christmas tree and her beach books. She'd added that Ms. Oakes' favorite color was pink. She'd loved the soft shade all her life but even more so when her daughter was born.

That sentence stopped me in my tracks. I hadn't known Ms. Oakes had a daughter. The woman kept to herself and didn't discuss her personal life—at least, not with me. I went back to reading.

Sienna said Ms. Oakes' daughter lives in Washington, and "it makes her sad that she doesn't get to see her often."

I wondered if Ms. Oakes and her daughter had quarreled and were estranged, or if they wanted to see each other more often but either time or money presented a roadblock. Thinking Sienna might have the answer, I put some money in an envelope and went upstairs to Antiquated Editions.

I found Ford sitting behind the counter looking down at his phone and Sienna perched primly on a chair in front of one of the shelves drawing in her notebook. I briefly wondered if she was making illustrations for Ella and Frank.

"Are you looking for an enthralling read?" Ford asked me.

"Maybe, but I'm mainly here to pay my brilliant detective." I handed Sienna the envelope, which contained double the amount we'd agreed upon. I was both surprised and impressed that she didn't immediately tear open the envelope.

"Thank you," she said. "Were you satisfied with the quality of my work?"

"Very much so. I do, however, have a follow-up question." I lowered my voice in case Ms. Oakes should happen to come out of her office. "Did you get the feeling Ms. Oakes and her daughter got along, or do you think maybe they don't want to see each other?"

"I'm not sure about the daughter, but I believe Ms. Oakes wants to see her," Sienna said. "But Ms. Oakes' mom is in a nursing home, and that's expensive."

"Wait—Ms. Oakes' mom is in a nursing home?" I asked.

"Yes." Furrowing her brow, she said, "I thought I put that in the report."

"You probably did, and I missed it. I'll read through it again." I nodded. "What else did she say that gave you the impression she wants to see her daughter?"

"Only that managing this building isn't easy either. It's a worry for her because one of the spaces has been vacant for months."

That I knew, but I didn't want to interrupt Sienna again.

"She thinks that if she doesn't get somebody in that space soon, she's afraid the building owners might feel like she's not doing a good job and fire her." Sienna poked out her bottom lip slightly. "Then who knows when she'd get to visit her daughter."

"Huh." I leaned against a display case that housed— among other things—a first edition of C. S. Lewis's *The Lion, the Witch and the Wardrobe*. "I never dreamed Ms. Oakes had so much on her mind."

"Me, either," Ford said. "I just thought she was an old grump."

Actually, so did I; but I didn't want to admit that in front of Sienna. She obviously had someone setting a good example for her as far as manners went, and I didn't want to do anything to discourage her. I thanked Sienna again for doing such a terrific job and said I'd see them both later.

I'd have said hello to Jason, but I heard someone in his studio and thought it likely he had a client with him.

When I went back downstairs, Max was sitting on the floor beside Jazzy, who was rolling over onto her back and stretching all four paws.

"Zoe asked that you call her when you get time," Max said.

"All right. Did you know Trish Oakes has a daughter?"

"There are photos in her office of a young woman I assumed was her daughter, but that's about the extent of my knowledge." Max stood.

"Sienna also told me Ms. Oakes' mother is in a nursing home."

Arching a brow, Max asked, "Winter Garden?"

"I don't know, but I intend to find out." I took out my phone. "Let's call Zoe."

As it turned out, Zoe wanted to come work on hats this afternoon.

"My friend, Stacy, can drop me off, if you don't mind taking me back home," she said.

"I can do that, provided you've cleared everything with your mom."

"I have. Do you want to call her?" I could hear the exasperation in her voice.

"No. I trust you," I said.

"And Mom trusts Stacy. She's a year older than I am, and she's the only one of my friends Mom will let me ride with."

"All right. Max and I will see you soon."

I stashed my phone in my dress pocket and spread the lining material for Ruby's coat out on the worktable so I could pin the pattern pieces to it.

Max looked wistfully at the royal blue silk. "This coat is going to be magnificent."

"I'll let you try it on when it's finished."

When I put a garment on the dress form, Max was able to superimpose herself onto the mannequin, thus "trying on" the piece. It was fun.

"Maybe you can let Zoe try it too," she said. "She and Ruby Mills are the same size, and I think Zoe would get a kick out of it."

"Me, too." I smoothed out the fabric and pinned a pattern piece in place. "You seem a little down."

"I have Dwight on my mind…and Dot. As a girl, Dot adored this time of year. I can only imagine how special she'd try to make the holidays for her children."

"Have you spoken with Dwight about his traditions growing up?" I asked, thinking maybe Dot kept some of the same ones Max and she had loved when they were little girls.

"Some. I'll talk with him more when I have a chance." Sighing, she added, "I miss my baby sister."

"I know."

"I'd hate myself if I let something horrible happen to her son."

"You won't," I said. "*We* won't." I prayed I could keep that promise.

Zoe got to the shop as I was finishing cutting out the lining for the coat. I gathered all the pattern pieces and set them aside.

"Ready to work on the hat?" I asked.

"I am," Zoe said.

She sat at one sewing machine, and I sat at the other—working together on our two separate hats. When we finished, I held her hat up for inspection. It looked good.

"I'm proud of the work you've done," I told her, with a broad smile. "And you should be too."

"I don't know." Zoe slowly shook her head. "Is my stitching off? I felt like I might have missed a stitch or something somewhere."

"If you did, I can't find it."

"Neither can I," Max said.

"What about my choice of embellishments?" Zoe asked.

"That rosette is the elephant's eyebrows!" Max put her hand on her chest. "I'd look marvelous in that hat. Come to think of it, so would you."

"You would," I agreed. "In fact, you should keep it and wear it. It's the first piece you created—you have to keep it and show it off."

"Plus, it's excellent advertising," Max said. "Once people see you in it, they're going to want their own."

"Yeah, right." Zoe rolled her eyes.

"Are you ready to get started on another one?" I asked.

"Sure."

"Then let's pick out your fabric." Together, we walked over to the shelf.

"I like both of these," Zoe said. "Help me choose."

"Why don't we cut out both? I have an older sewing machine at home—it's the one I learned to sew on, as a matter of fact—that I'll be happy to let you borrow," I said. "That way, you'll be able to work on the hats when you get home from school and finish your homework."

"We don't have homework this week—only tests."

Max placed an index finger at the corner of her mouth. "My favorite subjects in school were fashion and gossip, and I excelled in both."

Our laughter was interrupted by my cell phone.

I took it from my pocket and looked at the screen. It was Sally Jane.

"Hello, this is Amanda Tucker," I said.

"Amanda, it's Sally Jane." She took a deep breath. "I'm going to help."

Chapter Fourteen

As Zoe and I headed to her house after picking up the sewing machine and dropping off Jazzy, I urged her to tell her mom about our concerns over the nursing home.

"I know you believe she'll think you and Dwight are overreacting, but I'll tell her I'm concerned too—and so is a deputy with the Winter Garden Sheriff's Department."

Zoe was silent, so I glanced over at her. She nodded.

"I'll follow your lead," I said. "If you don't think she's in the mood to hear about it, I won't say a word."

"Okay. Thanks."

When we arrived at Zoe's small clapboard house, she held the door while I carried the sewing machine inside.

"What's that?" Maggie asked.

Maggie Flannagan looked perpetually tired. She was tall and thin, had dishwater blonde hair, and brown eyes that almost always held a hint of suspicion. Not that I could blame her—she'd had a hard life. Her husband had died in an accident when Zoe was so small that she could barely remember him now. Since then, she'd been the sole financial and parental support for Zoe. I imagined I'd be skeptical of anyone else in my daughter's life too if I were in Maggie's position.

"This is the machine I learned to sew on," I said. "I'm loaning it to Zoe so she can have more time to make the hats she wants to sell in the shop."

"I appreciate your doing that for Zoe—teaching her how to sew and all—but Zoe is going to pay you for the materials she uses before she takes one dime of profits from those hats."

Zoe huffed. "Mom! Of course, I'm going to pay Amanda for the stuff she gave me. You treat me like I'm a baby!"

"I'm only making sure you aren't taking advantage of Amanda's kindness," Maggie said.

"I'm not." She glared at her mother.

I thought maybe this was a good time to change the subject and ask Maggie about her dad. "I saw Dwight today."

To me, that was a good opening—if Zoe didn't want to raise our concerns to her mom, I could simply say I stopped by to say hello during lunch. Either way, it kept Maggie and Zoe from entering into a screaming match.

"Really?" Maggie squinted. "Why were you at the nursing home today? Is one of your family members there?"

"She went for *me*, Mom," Zoe said.

I had to hand it to her—the girl had pluck.

"I talked to Papaw before school, and he was upset because another one of his friends died," she continued. "I called Amanda and asked her to check on him."

"Why didn't you call me?" Maggie asked.

"Because you were at work!"

"So was she!" Maggie jerked her thumb in my direction.

Maggie had a fair point. Should I say something or keep my mouth shut?

"And he's *my* father!" Maggie added.

Definitely keep my mouth shut. At this point, I was sort of wishing I was somewhere else.

"But you act like he's crazy for being upset about his friends," Zoe said.

"I understand why he's sad his friends died. What I *don't* believe is that the nurses are killing them off." Maggie rubbed her forehead.

Zoe looked at me, her eyes imploring me to say something.

"I'm not sure anyone is killing off the nursing home residents," I said, choosing my words carefully, "but some concerns have been raised. My grandpa told me about a nurse who was anxious that her dad's medication wasn't being properly administered."

"What did they say when she spoke with them about it?" Maggie asked.

"Well, she didn't find out until her dad died. And he's the man who died last night, so I don't know what course of action she's pursuing," I said.

"We thought maybe I could leave my phone in Papaw's room to record what happens while no family or other visitors are there," Zoe said.

"No." Maggie shook her head. "Phones are too expensive to risk like that."

"I'll hide it, Mom. That's the point. I'll plug it in so the battery doesn't drain and—"

"I said no," Maggie said. "I don't care how well the phone is hidden, it could still fall and break. Or it could be discovered by one of the nurses. What if they realize we're spying on the nursing home and kicks Daddy out? Then what would we do? We'd have to uproot him and find another nursing home with an available bed—and this nursing home might not even be doing anything wrong."

"But what if they *are* doing something wrong? How are we going to know?" Zoe anchored her hands to her hips. "Are we just supposed to stand by and let them kill Papaw?"

"Stop being so melodramatic," Maggie said.

"There's a nursing home volunteer who expressed concern today about the residents' treatment," I said. "She works there three days a week and is going to see what she can uncover. Also, I don't mind going to see Dwight on my lunch break." I didn't normally take a lunch break, but I would if it would help ease Zoe's mind about her papaw.

Maggie stiffened. "I visit my dad every chance I get."

"I know you do," I said. "I'm also aware of how much you have going on and—"

"I don't need you to patronize me," she interrupted. "I appreciate everything you do for Zoe, but she's *my* daughter and Dwight is *my* dad. I'm capable of taking care of both of them." She walked over to the door. "Thank you for bringing the nursing home concerns to my attention. I'll take it from here."

"Mom, you can't talk to the nursing home people," Zoe said. "Papaw doesn't want you to."

"I'll talk everything over with Daddy tomorrow." She opened the door. "Thanks again for loaning Zoe the sewing machine, Amanda. Have a good evening."

I drove to Grandpa Dave's house before going home. One of the casserole crusaders was there. She was a bright-eyed woman with a headful of tight gray curls, and she was obviously disappointed when I crashed her party.

"Well, I'd better get going, Dave," she said. "I didn't realize you were expecting your granddaughter over. If you need any reheating instructions for the casserole, call me."

"All right, Willa. Thank you!" He smiled and waved goodbye to her from the porch. After she'd backed her car out of the driveway, he put an arm around me and steered me into the house. "The Lord directed your path tonight, Pup."

I laughed. "Don't you like Willa's cooking?"

"Oh, I *love* Willa's cooking—it's Willa I'm not that keen on." He motioned for me to follow him into the kitchen. "Have you had dinner?"

"Not yet."

"Good." He grinned. "We'll have some chicken casserole. We won't even have to reheat it because it's still hot."

I got out the plates while Grandpa got us some silverware and glasses.

"Where's Jazzy?" he asked.

"She's at home. I dropped her off and fed her before taking Zoe home." I explained about Zoe's friend dropping her off at the shop and how I'd loaned her a sewing machine so she could work on hats from home.

"Um, by the way, we might want to reconsider inviting Maggie to spend Christmas Eve with us."

"What happened?" He held up a pitcher. "Tea all right with you?"

I nodded before launching into the play-by-play of the skirmish between Zoe and Maggie.

"It sounds like you're lucky you escaped unscathed," he said.

"Well, I feel like I was a little scathed," I said. "Maggie all but threw me out of the house."

"Ah, she'll get over it. And we still have plenty of time before Christmas Eve. We'll play that one by ear."

After taking a drink of the tea he'd poured me, I said, "I wish I hadn't caused tension between Zoe and her mom."

Grandpa spooned casserole onto his plate. "I'd imagine it doesn't take much to cause tension between those two—kinda like you and your mother."

"The sad thing is those two don't have a wonderful guy like Dad to balance the scales and play mediator."

"No, but Zoe has a great relationship with her grandfather." He raised his glass. "Like someone else I know."

"I have the best grandpa ever," I said. "Everybody knows that."

"Agreed."

I tasted the casserole. "This is good. Maggie shut down the planted phone idea and basically told me to mind my own business."

"I know you aren't going to do that," Grandpa said.

"As well as I know you aren't going to mind your own business."

"And why would I? My business is boring." He gave a dramatic sigh. "Another day, another casserole."

Right. He wasn't fooling me. He was enjoying every moment of the casserole crusades.

Chapter Fifteen

I was kinda down in the dumps when I went into work on Tuesday morning. Glad to be the first person there again, I got my coffee, let Jazzy out of her carrier, and gave her food and water. Then I took out my laptop and sat at the worktable. I logged onto social media with the intention of finding Ms. Oakes' daughter.

I went to my boss's profile and scrolled through her feed until I could deduce that her daughter was named Krista Hollifield. Afraid Krista wouldn't see my message otherwise, I sent her a friend request with the following message:

Hi, Krista: I work with your mom at Shops on Main and drew her name for Secret Santa. I'd love to get the two of you together for Christmas—or, if that won't work

with your schedule, shortly thereafter. Please send me a
message so we can chat further. Thanks, Amanda Tucker

I'd just sent the message when Connie came into Designs on You. Her long blonde hair was in a single braid over her left shoulder, and she wore a red and white sweater over red jeans. She sort of reminded me of a candy cane; but being afraid that might not be the look she was going for, I didn't say so.

"Good morning," I said.

Connie was a gentle, artsy soul whose Delightful Home shop sold essential oils, tea blends, goat milk soaps and lotions, and other—well, delightful—things. She was married and had two children, a boy of around twelve—I believe—and a girl who was Zoe's age.

"Hello," Connie said. "Have you got a second?"

"Of course." I closed the laptop. "I was just sending a message to Trish Oakes' daughter explaining that I got her mom for Secret Santa and that I'd like to arrange a visit between them."

"Oh, that would be so nice." Connie sat on one of the sewing machine chairs. "I don't think Trish and Krista have seen much of each other since Krista took the job in Washington as a Senate page."

"She's a page? Wow, that's pretty prestigious."

"True, but it doesn't afford her a lot of time off, and I don't think it pays her enough to be able to hop a plane home often. And, of course, Trish can't go there because she has her mother to attend to." Connie gave her head a sad little shake. "Let me know when you hear back from Krista. I'd be happy to contribute money to buying a plane ticket. Some of the other vendors might chip in as well."

I was thinking they might do it just to get Ms. Oakes out of the building for a few days, but I didn't say so to Connie.

She lowered her voice before continuing. "I got Jason's name in the Secret Santa draw, and I hoped you might be able to give me a few ideas. I don't know him well at all."

"I imagine he'll be happy with anything you pick out," I said. "You have excellent taste. And there are lots of mugs and T-shirts out there for photographers."

"I did run across a darling vintage camera desk organizer, but I'd have to order it and don't think it would get here in time."

I got out my phone and showed her the customized leather camera strap I'd ordered Jason. "The canvas one he uses now has seen better days."

"Oh, that's beautiful." She smiled. "I'm so excited for the holidays this year. After some rocky months—with our losing Mark and then Sandra—I feel like the tide is turning our way."

"I do too." I didn't mention the things that were weighing on my mind this morning. She seemed happy, and I didn't want to bring her down.

After Connie left, Max appeared on the table in front of me. "What's with the face, Grace?"

"I'm a tad blue this morning."

"I could see that much. Tell me why," she said.

"Grandpa Dave told me yesterday that Mom and Dad aren't coming home for Christmas, and I feel like I caused a rift between Zoe and her mom last night."

"Nope. You didn't cause a rift." She wriggled her fingers for Jazzy, who'd hopped onto the table to sit near her. "I video chatted with Zoe last night after her mom went to bed. They argue fairly often, but they love each other and don't hold grudges."

"I'm worried Maggie thinks I'm trying to horn in too much on their lives—or, at least, Zoe's life." I put away my laptop and brought Ruby's coat to the table. I'd sewn the lining and pinned it to the fabric yesterday, and now I had to sew it to the coat.

"Zoe told me Maggie feels a little jealous of you and your relationship," Max said, getting off the table so Jazzy would stay off the fabric. "You're younger and more fun, and Maggie fears you have too much influence over her daughter."

"That's crazy. I don't want to compete with Maggie. I simply want to be a friend—to both of them." I turned around to the sewing machine.

"I know." Max moved over to my right, so I could see her better.

Jazzy followed and lay at Max's feet.

"Grandpa Dave wanted to invite Maggie and Zoe to his house for dinner on Christmas Eve," I said. "I told him after leaving their house last night that might not be such a great idea."

"And what did the silver fox say about that?"

"He said it's early yet and that we'll play it by ear."

She grinned. "He's a smart one. If there's a way to invite them that doesn't look like you think they're charity cases, Dave will find it."

"I know." I fed the material through the sewing machine.

"You're disappointed your parents aren't coming home for Christmas," Max said softly.

"I am." I lifted the presser foot and moved the fabric. "I might give Mom a call at lunchtime."

"You know, I'm surprised she told Dave but not you."

"I'm not," I said. "That's typical Mom—let someone else deliver the bad news."

"Yeah, but it's not like they aren't coming home at all, right? They're simply delaying their visit."

"That's true." I sewed another seam.

"Then why be sad?" she asked. "I know it's selfish of me, but I'm looking forward to spending Christmas with you, Dave, Zoe, and Dwight. And your parents being here might've thrown a wrench in some of my fun." She shrugged. "I haven't had anyone to spend Christmas with for decades. I'm looking forward to singing along to carols and watching your traditions take place."

I paused and looked up from my fabric. "Maybe we could incorporate some new traditions. What are some of the things you and your family used to do?"

"Mostly, we sat around and watched television." She smirked.

In America, television sets weren't released until 1938, eight years after Max's death.

"Okay, okay," she said. "Dot always baked some scrumptious goodies on Christmas Eve. Then mother would play the piano, and we'd sing carols. Before we went to bed, Daddy would read *T'was the Night Before Christmas*."

"That sounds really special."

"It was." Her voice took on a wistful tone. "I wish I'd better understood that then." She shook off the melancholy before adding, "I'm going to pop out for a while. Call your mother. Tell her you miss her. Your dad, too, of course, but I imagine he knows you miss him."

After Max left, I put on my headset and called my mom as I finished sewing up Ruby's beautiful coat.

I had quite a collection of buttons; and I was always adding to it, thanks to Etsy shops. I had several single buttons, but I preferred buttons I could buy more than one of. I'd recently discovered a shop that sold vintage Czech glass buttons and had procured four blue flower mandala buttons. I thought they would be beautiful on Ruby's coat.

I texted Ruby a photograph of the buttons to see what she thought of them.

Before I could put the buttons away, someone came into the reception area. I went to greet the newcomer and saw that it was Sarah Conrad, a petite brunette whose son, Joey, was a handful. And he was with her.

"Good morning, Sarah!" I said. "Hi, Joey."

"Hey." Joey went over and slouched in one of the navy wingback chairs.

"Hi, Amanda," Sarah said. "Joey had a dental appointment this morning, so I told him we'd stop a few places before I take him back to school." She gave him a pointed look. "We stopped at my place first to see how he behaves. He's promised me he doesn't have two ferrets hiding in his backpack this time."

Joey's ferrets—an albino named Biscuit and a brown one named Gravy—had wreaked havoc in my life on more than one occasion. Max didn't like them at all. She was afraid of what she called *weasels*—although what they could possibly do to her, I have no idea—and, like Jazzy, they could see her.

"Mom's gonna take us to lunch before I have to go back to school," Joey said. "I don't know why I have to go back at all. We're almost done."

"Right. You're almost done." She looked at me. "They finish up on Wednesday." Turning back to her son, she said, "That's why you need to go back today. You'll miss your friends when you're sitting at home for the next two weeks."

"I won't even get to talk to them until tomorrow when we have our party," he said.

Despite Sarah's assurance that Joey had no ferrets in his backpack, I noticed some telltale movement. Thinking—hoping—I was wrong, I asked Sarah what she was interested in today.

"I wanted to browse your ready-to-wear items to see if I can find something appropriate for a family party. My sister-in-law always wears the prettiest things, and—"

"And she tries to make Mom feel frumpy," Joey said.

"Joey!" Sarah exclaimed.

"Well, that's what you told Dad."

I had to put up a hand to hide my smile. "Then, Sarah, let's find you something fabulous."

We were looking at an emerald colored v-neck swing dress with three-quarter length sleeves when I caught a glimpse of white fur streaking past.

"Joey!" Her voice was one of exasperated warning.

"What? You asked if I had my ferrets—plural—and I don't. I just have Biscuit. I promised Gravy he could go to church tomorrow night."

While Sarah was debating Gravy's church visit with Joey, I hurried into the workroom to see what Biscuit was doing.

Naturally, the ferret had snapped up one of Ruby's buttons and was running with it back to Joey. Undoubtedly, the little thief wanted to hide its treasure in the backpack.

Jazzy was still in her bed but was stretching and considering giving chase to Biscuit. She apparently hadn't decided whether or not she wanted to play or continue napping.

Max popped in, saw the ferret, and screamed. Not that it mattered all that much, since I was the only one who could hear her. Oh, wait. Biscuit heard her.

The sleek white animal practically flipped around in mid-air and raced back toward Max, who was standing between the reception area and the atelier. The sight of Max brought Jazzy running to her rescue, so the cat and the ferret were having a stare-down between the feet of a ghost.

"Amanda, *do* something!" Max shouted.

"What should I do?" I asked.

"Oh, nothing, sweetie," Sarah said. "Just bear with us for a minute, and we'll catch the little rascal."

At least, Biscuit had dropped the button. I wanted to reach and swoop it up, but I was afraid the ferret might bite me. Despite the fact that I felt the ferrets and I were practically old friends by now, I hadn't had enough experience with ferrets to know what Biscuit might do if I tried to take back the button.

As if we didn't have enough excitement already, Sienna came barging into the workroom. "What's going on?" she asked.

Thankfully, she remembered to close the door behind her.

"I love ferrets!" She hurried over to Biscuit and dropped to her knees. "Hello."

"Her name is Biscuit," Joey said.

"Hi, Biscuit." She petted the ferret's head and it scampered into her arms. She stood and looked at Joey. "I'm Sienna. You wanna go see my uncle's bookstore? It's upstairs."

"Sure." He stood and accompanied Sienna through the workroom and out the door.

"I'll come back and talk with you in a few minutes, Amanda!" Sienna called before shutting the door.

"Do you think they'll be all right?" Sarah asked.

I retrieved Ruby's button. "They'll be fine."

Chapter Sixteen

Sarah sagged in relief when she heard Sienna and Joey tromping up the stairs, but then she turned to me with a worried frown. "What is there for them to get into up there? I know there's the bookstore, and—"

"They'll be all right," I reiterated. "Sienna has a good head on her shoulders. I even hired her—she's a detective, as a matter of fact—to find out what I could get the building manager for a Secret Santa gift. Until I read Sienna's report, I had no idea Ms. Oakes had a daughter who lives in D.C. or that her mother was in a nursing home."

Drawing in a breath, Sarah asked, "Which nursing home?"

"Winter Garden."

She shuddered. "I took my mom out of that place a couple of weeks ago."

"Really? Why?" I asked.

"Mom started telling me that one of the nurses was mean. I figured she was exaggerating and that she simply didn't get along with this particular nurse. But, just to make sure, I asked my husband to stop by the nursing home one morning around breakfast—a time when we never visited—because Mom had told me the nurse wouldn't help her sit up in bed so she could eat."

"That's terrible!"

"I know, and it was true." She blinked back tears. "He caught the nurse refusing to help Mom and telling Mom she wasn't their only patient. She was horribly disrespectful."

"What was the nurse's name?"

"Penelope," she said. "After sitting Mom up and helping her eat her breakfast, my husband took off work for the rest of the day and wouldn't leave the nursing home until he found Mom a bed at a nursing home here in Abingdon. We moved her that day."

"I'm glad you found a new place so easily. Is she happier there?"

"Much." Sarah shook her head. "The staff really cares for their residents. They informed us when we moved her that Mom had a really bad bedsore on her hip, but they've almost got it healed now. Plus, they have lots of special events for their members—they treat them like *people*."

"I'm sorry you had such a rotten experience with Winter Garden Nursing Home," I said. "I think I should—without mentioning any names—tell Ms. Oakes about your experience."

"Feel free to mention my name. I don't want anyone to go through what Mom did, and I don't mind discussing it with Ms. Oakes or anyone else our story might help." She looked at the green dress she'd been admiring before Biscuit got loose. "This is gorgeous. I'm going to try it on."

I waited while Sarah got changed. I was afraid that given Sarah's petite frame, the dress would need to be hemmed; but it was perfect.

"It looks as if it was made for you," I said.

She giggled as she spun around in front of the triple mirror. "It does, doesn't it? I love it!"

"Shall I ring it up for you?"

"Yes, please," she said.

As I was putting the dress in a garment bag for her, Sienna and Joey returned. Sienna was holding Biscuit, and Joey was carrying a book.

Holding up the book for his mom's inspection, he said, "Look what Uncle Ford gave me."

The book was *The Story of Doctor Doolittle* by Hugh Lofting.

"Let me pay for my dress, and we'll go back up and thank…Mr. Ford," Sarah said.

When the trio—quartet, if you count Biscuit—left, Max materialized.

"Did you hear what Sarah was saying about the nursing home?" I asked.

"I heard."

"What do you think I should do?" I walked over to sit at my desk. "Maggie is already upset with me for sticking my nose into her business, and Ms. Oakes has never welcomed my input on anything."

"Let me think." She went into the workroom.

I got up and followed her.

Max sat at the corner of the worktable where her tablet was currently plugged into an outlet charging. I was curious as to what she was doing; but before I could peep over her shoulder, Jason came into the room.

"Hi, beautiful. Check this out." He brought his camera over and showed me on the display screen images he'd captured of Sienna, Joey, and Biscuit.

"Those are adorable."

"I'd hoped Joey's mom hadn't left yet," he said. "I was going to print out a couple for her."

"I don't see how you two didn't pass each other on the stairs. She just went up to thank Ford for the book he gave Joey."

"I'll run back up and see if I can catch her." He gave me a quick kiss. "Can I take you to lunch today?"

"Absolutely."

When he left, I went over to see what Max was doing. She had one tab open to a rare coins webpage, and she had sent a video chat request to Dwight in another.

"Hello, ladies," he said, after accepting the request.

"Hi, Dwight. How are you doing today?" I asked.

"I'm finer than a frog hair split four ways," he said.

"No, he isn't," Max said. She told him how mean the nursing home staff—that Penelope, especially—was to Sarah Conrad's mother. "I want to get you out of that place."

"Aunt Max, I'm fine. Maggie wants me here, I can't afford to move even if I wanted to, and I don't have any bedsores—I have more mobility than a lot of the other residents."

"You might have more money than you think," Max murmured.

"What?" I asked.

"I don't think so," Dwight said.

"Darling, I'll talk with you later—there's something I need to do." She ended the video chat.

"Max, what are you up to?"

Ignoring me, she requested a video chat with Grandpa Dave. Within seconds, his face filled the screen of her tablet.

"Good afternoon, ladies. I was getting ready to make some lunch."

"What are you having?" I asked.

"Chicken salad on—"

"That's wonderful, darling," Max interrupted, "and I hope it's delicious, but I have something pressing to ask you."

"Anything," he said.

"Do you have the necessary tools to pull up and replace floorboards in a closet?" she asked.

"Max, what's going on?" I asked.

"Of course," Grandpa said. "Is it something you need done today?"

"Tonight," she said. "When everyone else—except you, Amanda—is gone."

He blew out a breath and searched my face. "What are you two up to, Pup?"

"I'm not up to anything, and Max won't tell me what's going on with her."

"It could be nothing, and I don't want to get Dwight's hopes up, but years ago, Daddy had a strongbox he kept hidden from Mother. It's in the room that's currently vacant—that used to be their bedroom."

"How do you know it's still there?" I asked.

"Because I keep my eye on that box. It was Daddy's." She lifted her chin. "It was important to him, and it's important to me. Anytime this house was sold or bought or renovated, I watched to make sure no one got close to Daddy's box. If they started to, I'd make something happen to scare them away."

"What's in it?" I first imagined all sorts of treasures, and then I immediately imagined a whole lot of dust and pennies.

"I don't know if there will be anything worthwhile in there, but I have to think there is," Max said.

"It'll be worthwhile to you," Grandpa said gently.

"Yes, but I want it to be valuable to Dwight— something Zoe can sell and get enough money out of that she can move him out of that dreadful nursing home."

Grandpa and I exchanged worried glances.

"How are we going to get into the vacant space after hours?" I asked. "Ms. Oakes always makes sure it's locked."

"Hire the spy to get the key," Max said.

"But—" I was interrupted by Jason returning.

Naturally, he couldn't see Max, but he came over to speak with Grandpa Dave.

"Hey, Dave! How're you doing?"

"I'm great. How are you?"

"Good. I'm getting ready to take your granddaughter to lunch," Jason said.

"Great." Grandpa Dave grinned. "I was just about to grab a bite myself. You two have fun."

"Thanks." I walked over to get my jacket.

"Aren't you going to cut off your tablet?" Jason asked.

"It'll go off on its own," I said, looking over my shoulder to see Max impatiently waiting for us to leave so she could talk with Grandpa Dave some more.

What in the world was in that box? And how much were Grandpa Dave and I going to have to risk to find out?

Chapter Seventeen

Jason and I went to lunch at our favorite sandwich shop. I ordered chicken salad, and he ordered ham and Swiss on rye. As we sipped our sodas and waited for our food, I told him about my dilemma.

"Should I tell Ms. Oakes and Maggie Flannagan what I learned from Sarah Conrad? Or should I butt out?" I asked.

"What did Dave say?"

I realized Jason thought that was why I was video chatting with Grandpa. Oh, well, it beat him knowing the truth—that we were discussing breaking into a locked room and removing floorboards in a closet because our ghost friend wanted us to.

"Neither of us is sure what to do," I said. "While I don't want to intrude on anyone's privacy or falsely accuse the nursing home staff of negligence, I'd want to know if someone had concerns about the place if Grandpa lived there. I'd at least want to exercise more vigilance."

"Don't worry. Ryan is actively investigating the nursing home. If there's anything shady going on there, he'll find it." He took a deep breath. "Let's talk about something more pleasant."

"Okay." I drew the word out, wondering why he'd take a deep breath as if he were dreading whatever *pleasant* subject he wanted to discuss.

He smiled. "So, do you have plans on Saturday?"

"I have to work until noon."

"I know, but this would be after that."

I gave him a playful side-eye. "Mr. Logan, are you asking me on a date?"

"In a way." He laughed. "I'm trying to invite you to my grandparents' Christmas party. It's a potluck, and it would give you an opportunity to meet my family in a laidback setting."

Now I understood why he'd been hesitant. "And I'd be meeting your entire family at once. Sure, that's laidback."

"I understand if you don't want to go," he said.

"Oh, no, I do." I felt this was a crucial point in our relationship, and I *did* want to go. "It just makes me a little nervous, that's all."

"No need to be anxious. They'll love you."

Remembering Max wanting Grandpa Dave and me to break into the vacant shop, I hoped he and I wouldn't be spending Saturday evening in jail. Surely, we could make bail by then.

When I got back to Designs on You, Max was waiting to chat.

"How was lunch?" she asked.

"Jason wants me to meet his family on Saturday." I blew out a breath. "Not just his parents, but his entire family. His grandparents are having a Christmas potluck."

She squeezed her hands together at her chest. "How exciting! He wants to introduce you to the whole clan! This romance is getting serious."

"What should I take to the potluck?"

"Who cares?" She flicked her wrist. "No one will care what you bring—they'll be too busy checking out what you wear and how you look at Lover Boy."

"Great. Thanks for that. That brings me to my next question—what should I wear?"

"Something fabulous, of course. But we have the rest of the week to plan your Saturday," she said. "Let's talk about tonight. I'm thinking our best course of action might be to have that little spy kid to lift the key."

"Max—"

"It would be exhilarating for her! Plus, it would be good practice for her if she truly does want to become a spy or a detective."

"No," I said. "I refuse to let a child take part in something that could end up getting Grandpa Dave and me arrested. But I did come up with another idea over lunch."

I took out my phone. Grandpa Dave wasn't showing up on social media, so I gave him a call.

"Hi, Pup. You aren't engaged or anything, are you?"

"No. Why would you think that?" I asked.

"Well, you're calling me right after lunch with your young man. I thought you might have news."

I did have, but I'd fill him in on that later. Hopefully, he'd be more help than Max had been in deciding what to take to the potluck. "I called to see if you'd be willing to pretend you have a friend interested in the space upstairs."

"Well, I've already committed to pulling up floorboards in a closet, so sure, I can handle that."

Max giggled.

"Tell that specter she's going to be the death of us all," he added.

"Never, darling," she said.

"Ms. Oakes is always out of here by 5:15 every evening," I said. "If you were to show up at the end of the day—say around five o'clock—and ask to see the space, we can assure her that we'll lock up after you take some measurements. According to Sienna, Ms. Oakes is desperate to get that space leased, so I'm guessing she'll concede to our offer to lock up."

"You're good. I'll get there a little before five and wait in the parking lot. That way, if she leaves early, I'll be there to intercept her."

"Dave, you're an absolute treasure," Max said.

"I doubt Ms. Oakes would see it that way if she knew what we were doing," he said.

"I hate deceiving her," I said. "And now that I know about her mom, I'm guessing she goes to the nursing home on her way home every day. I'll do my best to find someone to rent that space after this."

"Me, too, Pup."

"Me, three!" Max chimed in.

I rolled my eyes at her. "If Ms. Oakes won't leave us alone to retrieve the box, then we'll have to think of something else."

"Did you decide whether or not to tell Ms. Oakes and Maggie about Sarah's allegations?" Grandpa asked.

"I'm going to talk with Ms. Oakes, maybe when we meet with her after work," I said. "Maggie is already aware of our concerns, and I'm afraid saying anything more would only make matters worse. But I feel obligated to broach the subject with Ms. Oakes."

"Especially since giving her the willies about the nursing home will make her more willing to get out of here and leave you the key to the empty space." Max winked. "Excellent thinking, darling."

I opened my mouth to protest but figured it was pointless. Instead, I told Grandpa I'd see him soon.

I had finished Ruby's coat and hat and called her to let her know it was ready. She'd be picking it up this afternoon. I put the coat and hat on the mannequin to let Max try it on like I'd promised her.

Moving the mannequin in front of the three-way mirror, I asked Max if she was nearby.

She appeared by my side. "I'm here. I was simply resting up for our exciting evening."

I was dreading our so-called exciting evening, but I didn't say so. "This won't take but a moment. I thought you'd want to see yourself in Ruby's coat and hat before she comes to get it."

"You know I do!" She superimposed herself onto the mannequin and gasped. "Isn't this incredible?"

"You look gorgeous," I said.

"Who are you talking to?"

I turned, surprised to see Sienna. "I didn't hear you come in."

"I did it quiet, like a detective would. Who are you talking to?"

"The…um…the coat. I'm really happy with the way it turned out."

"It is very pretty," Sienna said, "but do you always talk to your clothes?"

I shrugged. "Sometimes, I do."

She gave me a nod that made me think if the detective business didn't work out, she might want to consider being a therapist. "I didn't get to talk with you when I came by earlier this morning because I got busy with Joey and Biscuit."

"Well, it's always nice to make new friends, don't you think?"

"Yes, it is. And Joey and I exchanged phone numbers, so we can be friends from now on even though we go to different schools," she said.

"That's great."

"Yeah. Anyway, I wanted to follow up with you and see if there's anything else you need me to do."

"No," I said. "I'm delighted with the thorough job you did, and I'll certainly hire you again if and when the need arises."

"Great. Thanks." She sat on one of the sewing machine chairs and began spinning around. "So, Amanda, what's your favorite color?"

"I can't say I have a favorite," I said. "I like them all—separately and in various combinations—"

"When you're not here working, what do you enjoy doing?" she asked.

It dawned on me that she was working on her report for the person who drew my name for the Secret Santa gifts. Smiling slightly, I walked away from the mirror, leaving Max to admire herself a little longer, and took a seat beside Sienna. Answering the diminutive detective's questions would be a good distraction from the nail-biting evening that lay before Grandpa Dave and me.

Chapter Eighteen

R uby had been delighted with her coat and hat. I was glad she was still a satisfied customer, and I was also pleased with the boost to my bank account. I waved to Ruby from the window as she walked down the sidewalk to her car.

Max materialized and offered up a sad little sigh. "I looked beautiful in that coat."

"You certainly did."

"I'm sorry Zoe didn't get to try it on," she said.

"Me, too. Have you spoken with her since this morning?"

"No." She gave her head a vehement shake. "I've been staying off social media because I don't want to talk with her yet."

"I'm hesitant to talk with her too. Despite what you said earlier, I still feel like I might've caused trouble between Zoe and her mom." I looked at the clock. It was creeping ever closer to five o'clock. "What are you expecting us to find in your dad's strongbox?"

"I don't really know. I haven't looked inside it in more than eighty years. Daddy smoked, but he hid it—or tried to—from Mother. Anything he didn't want her to know about, he secreted away in that box." She smiled. "Sometimes when she and Dot were at the store or somewhere, he'd get out the box and show me all his little treasures. That's what he called them—little treasures. He said Dot and I were his big treasures."

"Did he ever share what was in the box with Dot?" I asked.

"I don't think so. I was Daddy's pet. Dot was Mother's."

"Can't you recall *anything* that was in the box?" I pressed her because I was not only curious about its contents but afraid that whatever was in the box wouldn't be worth the risk Grandpa and I were taking to get it.

"There were a few coins, some cigarette packs, and—" She crossed her fingers. "—hopefully, some money."

I doubted there was enough money—or anything else in the box so valuable—to allow Dwight to move to another nursing home, but I didn't tell Max that. If nothing else, if Grandpa and I could extricate the box from its hiding place without suffering dire consequences, it would be worth it to let Max enjoy some nostalgia.

Glancing over at the window looking out onto the parking lot, I saw Grandpa pull in and shut off his engine. When he didn't get out of the truck right away, I guessed he wanted to come into the building as late as possible to avoid having Ms. Oakes stay until he was finished measuring the room.

Frank and Ella crossed the lot to get into their car. Frank waved to Grandpa, and Grandpa got out of the truck to speak with Frank for a minute.

As Grandpa carried his small red toolbox toward the building, Frank and Ella got into their car. I thought, *Two down. Three, actually, since Jason left earlier this afternoon for an appointment.*

I hoped Connie and Ford had no reason to stay late. Since Ford probably needed to get Sienna home, and Connie tried to never miss dinner with her family, I doubted they'd be here for much longer.

When Grandpa came in the back entrance, Max and I went to meet him.

"Hello, Pup." He winked at Max. "You must've seen me coming."

"I did. We should hurry on up to Ms. Oakes' office before she leaves."

Ms. Oakes was coming out of her office with her keys in her hand when Grandpa and I—and Max, of course—got to the top of the stairs.

"I'm sorry to bother you, Ms. Oakes," I said. "Have you got a second? My grandpa and I would like to speak with you."

She pressed her lips together firmly before asking, "Can't it wait until tomorrow?"

Grandpa crossed the hall to where Ms. Oakes was standing. "I'm Dave Tucker, Ms. Oakes. We've met previously, but you'd have no reason to remember an old coot like me."

"I remember you, Mr. Tucker, but I'm in a terrible hurry."

"I realize that, but I'd just like to take a few measurements while I'm here, if it isn't too much trouble," he said.

"Measurements of what?"

Jerking his head toward the vacant space, he said, "I know someone who might be interested in the space you have available for lease."

"Oh, really?" Ms. Oakes quickly unlocked her door. "I have all the dimensions you need." She dropped her purse onto a chair, went around the desk, and began rifling through the top drawer. "Here you go."

Grandpa looked at the paper, which gave the shop's square footage, length, and width. "I appreciate this, but I need a bit more information. I need to know the number of electrical outlets and how far apart they are, how close the outlets are to the center of the room, the amount of storage space—"

"My goodness, what kind of shop does your friend have?" she asked.

"He doesn't yet." Grandpa chuckled. "But he's thinking hobbies."

"A hobby shop." Ms. Oakes nodded. "That sounds charming."

"So, could I take some measurements?" he asked.

"Sure, but—"

Max waved her hands and then mimed a mother rocking her baby in her arms.

"I understand your mom is in Winter Garden Nursing Home." I realized I'd interrupted the woman, but I needed to have my say before she took off. I knew Max wanted me to tell Ms. Oakes about Sarah's concerns so Ms. Oakes would go on and leave, but I wanted to warn her because I was worried about all the residents there.

Ms. Oakes looked at her watch. "Yes, my mother is in the nursing home. What does that have to do with anything?"

"I have a client who was in today—Sarah Conrad— and she told me she recently moved her mother out of that facility." I explained the reason behind Sarah's actions.

"That is worrisome, but I'm sure it's an isolated case." She looked at Grandpa Dave. "Are you sure you can't simply come back and get the measurements tomorrow?"

"If you wouldn't mind allowing me to borrow the key to the vacant space," I said, "I can let Grandpa take his measurements and then give the key back to you tomorrow morning."

She sighed. "Fine." She took the key from the corkboard in her office where she had the keys to each space individually labeled and hung on a small hook. She handed me the key. "I'm holding you personally responsible for this key."

Max contorted her face into a grimace and shook an index finger at me.

"I understand." I had to look away from Max—which wasn't easy, since she was standing directly behind Ms. Oakes—to keep from laughing.

Ford and Sienna came out of Antiquated Editions as we stepped back into the hallway from Ms. Oakes' office.

"Everybody have a good evening," Ford said.

"You too," I called. "Bye, Sienna."

"Bye." She marched down the stairs beside Ford who insisted, to her dismay, that she hold his hand and the handrail. "I'm not a child, Uncle Ford."

Grandpa and I shared a grin, and I could've sworn I even saw Ms. Oakes' lips twitch.

I wasn't sure whether or not Connie had left yet, but soon we would have the entire upstairs to ourselves.

Ms. Oakes waited while I unlocked the door to the vacant space for Grandpa.

He went inside and took a measuring tape from the toolbox. "Pup, can you take some notes for me?"

"Of course." I went inside, wondering why I hadn't thought of that before and where I could get paper and a pen.

As if reading my mind, Grandpa said, "I keep a notebook and a carpenter's pencil right in the top of my toolbox."

Ms. Oakes watched as Grandpa went to the first outlet and began to measure. Then, apparently convinced we were doing nothing nefarious, she said, "Goodbye, then. Amanda, be sure to lock that door back securely and take care of the key."

"I will, Ms. Oakes. Thank you."

As soon as Ms. Oakes started down the steps, Max went to the closet. "Come on! Get over here!"

"Give me a minute," he said.

Afraid Ms. Oakes might've overheard, I said, "Sorry. I have a lot to do this evening."

Grandpa whispered to Max, "Go see if Connie has left and make sure Ms. Oakes is gone."

"Okay." She popped out.

Within seconds, she'd returned. "Connie is still here, but she's gathering up her things. Right now, she's chatting with Ms. Oakes. She didn't have time for us, but she can make time to talk with Connie." She rolled her eyes. "Anyway, I'm guessing they'll walk out together."

After Max gave us the all-clear, I shut the door and we went over to the closet.

"It's this board right here," Max said. "I remember it because it has those two black dots in the wood. See?"

There were indeed two small dots on one of the floorboards.

"We're sure this is the right one?" Grandpa asked.

Max nodded. "Hurry! I can hardly wait!"

As Grandpa gently pried the board up with a small pry bar, we heard footsteps on the stairs.

He and I froze. Max ran through the door to see who was coming.

She poked her head through the wall. "It's Jason!"

Grandpa stepped away from the closet and closed the door.

"Get in here," I hissed to Max, remembering belatedly that he couldn't see her.

Nevertheless, she stepped on into the room. "Nuts! Now we'll have to wait until he's gone."

"Maybe if we're quiet, he won't know we're in here," Grandpa whispered.

We heard Jason go into his studio and move around. He was probably putting away his equipment.

"We should do something other than stand here looking guilty in case he does come in." I took the measuring tape and moved over to the window.

Sure enough, seconds later, Jason knocked and then came on into the room. "Hey, there! I saw lights when I pulled in." He gave me a mischievous grin. "Are you moving upstairs to be closer to me?"

"No." I chuckled. "Grandpa is taking some measurements because he might know of someone who'd like to lease the space." I justified the fib by telling myself that Grandpa might know of someone.

"Do you need any help, Dave?" he asked.

"Nope. We're almost finished."

I walked over to Jason, linked my arm through his, and walked him into the hall. "I'm looking forward to meeting your family this weekend. When I get home, I'm going through my recipe box to see what I might bring."

"You don't have to bring anything," he said. "They'll be happy just to meet you."

"Now, you know I'm going to bring something." I led him out of Grandpa's sight so I could give him a kiss.

"You can bring that—but not to share."

I smiled. "Never. Hug Rascal for me."

He glanced toward the door, apparently made sure Grandpa wasn't coming, and kissed me again. "See you tomorrow morning then." He headed down the steps.

When I went back into the vacant shop, Max and Grandpa had their backs to me with their arms around themselves to make it look as if they were being embraced by someone else.

"Oh, ha-ha," I said. "Very mature."

Turning toward me with a smile, Grandpa said, "I heard something about meeting Jason's family?"

"Yeah. Jason asked me over lunch. His grandparents are having a potluck."

He and Max shared a knowing look.

"What?" I spread my hands. "Could we please just get back to the task at hand?"

"I'll make sure Romeo has left the balcony," Max said.

Grandpa went back to the closet, removed the box, and fixed the floor back. He'd secured the board so well it looked as if it had never been tampered with.

"That's impressive work," I said.

"Romeo has left the building and ventured forth into the night," Max reported.

"Good. Let's get out of here." I opened the door.

Grandpa retrieved the box, closed the closet door, and came to stand beside me. He surveyed the room. "Looks good, don't you think?"

"Nothing out of place," I said. "You wouldn't know we'd done anything except take a few measurements. And if you weren't aware of it, you wouldn't know we'd done that."

"Well, we didn't take many," he said.

I locked the door back, and we went downstairs to Designs on You. I put the key to the vacant space on the mantle before making sure both entrances to Designs on You were locked.

Always delighted to see Grandpa, Jazzy wound around his ankles. When he placed the box onto the workroom table, she hopped up.

"Apparently, we aren't the only ones eager to know what's in here," Grandpa said.

The box didn't have a lock, but it hadn't been opened in so long, it took some effort on Grandpa's part. I picked up Jazzy to keep her out of his way. Finally, the lid was off.

Frankly, at first glance, it looked like it was filled with junk. Inside were the cigarette packs Max had mentioned.

"Holy cow!" Grandpa picked up one of the cigarette packs. "Carolina Brights." His eyes widened. "There's a card in this."

"Uh-huh," Max said. "Baseball cards. Mother thought they were frivolous, but Daddy loved them. He always put them back in their packs to keep them nice."

I'd heard old baseball cards could be valuable, but Grandpa was removing the card from the pack as if he were Indiana Jones and he was getting ready to see the Holy Grail.

The card was a #33 Chief Bender. I'd never heard of a Chief Bender. I guess the card wasn't important after all.

"Chief Bender." Grandpa gaped at the card. "Well, I'll be."

"Was he famous?" I asked.

"Indeed he was." He carefully slid the card back into the packet. "Let's see what else we've got here."

Along with a number of baseball cards—most of which featured players I'd never heard of but with whom Grandpa was impressed—were a 1904 Morgan silver dollar, several silver peace dollars dated 1921 through 1928, some wheat pennies, standing liberty quarters, and buffalo nickels.

But the last thing Grandpa lifted out of the box even made me gasp. It was a 1921 Babe Ruth baseball card, and it was autographed in blue ink.

"Your dad met Babe Ruth?" Grandpa asked incredulously.

"Yes, and so did I. We went down to the train station in Bristol in April of 1922 to meet him." She laughed. "There was the awfulest crowd of people there. And the Bambino was ever so handsome. I caught his eye, but Daddy nixed that—after he got the autograph, of course."

Following a moment of stunned silence, Grandpa said, "I have a friend who is a certified appraiser of collectibles and memorabilia. Max, do you trust me?"

"With my life—or, you know, I would if I were living. Why?"

"I'm going to get these things appraised, and I believe my friend can help me find a buyer," he said.

"But how can we use the proceeds to help Dwight?" I asked.

"When Dwight remembers where he put that box of memorabilia his grandfather left him, he'll give it to Zoe," Max said. "Then she can use it however she wishes."

"She can, as long as Maggie agrees," I said.

"Phooey on that," Max said. "I want Dwight and Zoe to be in charge of the money."

"Then maybe we can set up a living trust for Dwight with Zoe as the beneficiary." Grandpa put everything back in the box and replaced the lid. "But we're putting the cart before the horse. Let's find out the value of the box's contents before we do anything else."

"Should we tell Zoe?" I asked.

"No."

Grandpa and Max spoke at once.

"Great minds, silver fox," she said. "After we know what we've got, we'll tell her. That way, we won't get her hopes up for nothing."

Chapter Nineteen

When we got out to the parking lot, Grandpa Dave told me to take Jazzy on home and get her squared away.

"I'll pick us up some burgers and fries and meet you at your house," he said.

"Sounds good." I kissed his cheek. "Be careful."

"You, too, Pup."

I went home, slipped off my shoes, fed Jazzy, and went through the day's mail. Most of the mail was junk, but I still took the time to flip through a catalog for beauty products.

Grandpa was somber when he arrived with our food.

"Are you okay?" I asked.

Nodding, he placed the bag and the drink tray onto the kitchen table.

"Thank you for dinner." I was treading carefully, knowing he'd tell me what he had on his mind when he was ready.

We sat down at the table, and he looked across at me. "That box makes me nervous. When I got into the truck, I immediately put the box under the passenger seat; and when I got here, I locked the doors. That's the first time I've ever felt obliged to lock my vehicle at this house before."

"Grandpa, it's always a good idea to keep your truck locked—you know that."

"That's true, but I've never been responsible for what amounts to someone's life savings in a box—Max's life's savings."

"The box was hidden upstairs and protected by a ghost—which is pretty cool when you think about it—for well over eighty years," I said. "Why are you worried something will happen to it now?"

"Because we've moved it...changed the dynamic or status quo or whatever you want to call it. Max can't watch out over it anymore. It's up to me."

"Relax." I chuckled. "I feel like our roles are reversed this evening—I'm being the grandparent for a change. Besides, it isn't Max's life's savings. It's a box of her Dad's trinkets. I'm sure they're worth *something*, but I doubt it will be enough to make a difference in the big scheme of things."

"That's just it," he said. "I phoned my friend the appraiser on the way here. She thinks that box could be worth a life-changing amount of money."

Before I could wrap my mind around his statement about life-changing money, I asked, "Where did you tell her you got the box?"

"I said it belongs to a friend who's in a nursing home and that the box was his grandfather's," he said. "The truth is always best, as long as the part about his deceased Aunt Max giving Dwight the box is omitted."

As we ate our food, Grandpa decided to change the subject.

"Tell me about this potluck at Jason's grandparents' home," he said.

"I'm nervous about it—I can tell you that. Although Jason seems to think this way will be more laidback than meeting his parents one-on-one."

"I agree. There will presumably be a lot of people at this potluck, so you shouldn't feel like you're under a magnifying glass."

"What dish should I take?" I asked.

"Banana pudding."

I scrunched up my face. "Really? I love banana pudding, but I was thinking I should take something fancier."

"Make it with meringue instead of whipped cream, and you'll impress the whole family."

"I'm not sure I can make it with the meringue," I said.

He grinned. "I can."

Was I really going to let my grandfather make the dish I was taking to Jason's family's potluck? Maybe we could make it together. That would work, wouldn't it?

"Hey, I think Zoe gets off school early tomorrow. If she comes by the shop, what should I tell her about the box—if anything?" I asked.

"I'm meeting with the appraiser in the morning and will come by the shop as soon as we're finished."

Max and I were on pins and needles as we waited for Grandpa to come to the shop the next morning.

"I spoke with Dwight last night over social media," Max said. "I told him I found a box of trinkets that belonged to his grandfather. Dwight remembered Daddy and still has a few coins Daddy gave him from the year he was born."

"That's sweet," I said.

"Yeah. I told him there were some coins in the box I found and that there were also some baseball cards." She laughed. "Dwight told me how Daddy used to regale him with the story of how he'd met Babe Ruth when the Bambino came to Bristol. I know Dwight became the apple of Daddy's eye. I'd have loved to have known Dwight when he was a little boy—to have been able to see him with Daddy and with Dot."

"I'm sure Dwight—or maybe Maggie—has some photographs." I wished for the umpteenth time I could put a hand on Max's shoulder. "Zoe would be happy to share them with you."

"I know." Max lifted her eyes to the ceiling to try to keep from tearing up. It didn't work. "I hope I can find a way to help protect my nephew."

"I believe you already have," I told her.

I had created Marsha Billings' muslin pattern yesterday after finishing Ruby Mills' coat, and she breezed in for her first fitting.

She was wearing a plaid scarf and she tossed it over her shoulder dramatically. "Shall I have Mrs. Patmore make us some tea?" Marsha's British accent was as bad as you might imagine.

Mine was probably worse when I responded, "But, of course, darling."

She laughed. "So, let's see this muslin."

I brought out the semi-transparent garment.

Marsha placed her well-manicured hand over her chest. "Oh, my! Granny would be incensed!"

"Wouldn't she though?" I led Marsha behind the Oriental screen and waited while she changed into the muslin.

She stepped out and spread her arms. "Ta-da!"

Max laughed. "I didn't particularly like this bird when she first landed here, but she's growing on me."

"It's a perfect fit," I said. "Your gown is going to be beautiful."

Sienna popped into the workroom then and didn't seem as surprised as I'd have imagined she might be to see a half-naked woman standing in front of the screen.

"Hi." To Marsha, she asked, "Why are you wearing a see-through paper bag? Is it a costume?"

Marsha stepped behind the screen. "Anything you need, Amanda, before I get dressed again?"

"No, Marsha. I'll make the gown to the muslin pattern, and it will look amazing."

"What are you doing?" Sienna called out to Marsha.

"Getting my clothes back on," Marsha retorted. "Is that all right with you?"

"Sure, but I mean, what were you doing in the weird outfit?" she asked. "Are you playing a paper bag in a Christmas play or something?"

Max was getting far too much amusement out of the situation.

Ignoring the ghost and concentrating on the pint-sized spy, who really needed to learn to knock before entering a workroom, I said, "What Ms. Billings was wearing is called a muslin. The muslin lets me know—before I cut into expensive fabric—that I've got the measurements correct so that I can now make Ms. Billings' actual gown."

"When do you think that will be ready?" Marsha asked, stepping out from behind the screen fully dressed.

"Within the next couple of days if your fabric arrives in time." I said a silent prayer that the material I ordered would arrive today.

"What you said about the muslin makes sense, I guess," Sienna said, "but that really would make a cool paper bag costume. Just something to keep in mind."

"Actually, my husband might like it." Marsha winked at me.

"Why? Do you think he'd make a good paper bag?" Sienna asked.

Max doubled over with laughter, and I had to turn and suddenly look at something really fascinating in the other room.

At last, we saw Grandpa pull into the parking lot. Max and I raised our squeezed fists in excitement.

"Wonder what she said?" Max asked.

"We'll find out soon enough."

Actually, it *wasn't* soon enough because Grandpa met with delay after delay. First, we heard Frank come out of Everything Paper to shoot the breeze. Before Frank was finished chatting up Grandpa, Trish Oakes hurried down the stairs.

Max poked her head through the wall so she could listen and report back to me.

"Crabapple Oakes is asking him about the space," Max said. "Does his friend want to come by and see it?"

"What's he saying?" I asked.

"Says he'll let her know. She's not happy about it, but Dave is charming, and she needs to lease the space, so she's not being rude."

Finally, Grandpa made it into the shop.

"Well?" Max asked.

"If my friend can find buyers, she thinks we're looking at over a quarter of a million dollars."

Chapter Twenty

Not knowing what to do with the information that Dwight could be gaining such a windfall, we decided our best course of action was to present the information to the man himself and get his opinion. Dwight appeared to be in complete control of his faculties, except for feeling paranoid—which we'd concluded wasn't an absurd suspicion after all—and not realizing his Aunt Max was a ghost. So, Grandpa and I headed out to Winter Garden Nursing Home.

Remembering Zoe's story about the coconut cake Dot had used to bribe Dwight into asking a girl to a dance, I had Grandpa swing by the grocery store. I had no delusions that the slice of cake I bought at the store could rival Dot's, but it still looked pretty tasty. And I felt that celebrations called for cake.

Grandpa and I found Dwight finishing up his lunch, so our timing was excellent.

"This is a nice surprise," Dwight said. "I'm sorry I don't have any lunch left to offer you."

"That's all right," I said. "I have dessert to offer you." As I handed him the clear container of cake, I told him Zoe had entertained us with the coconut cake story.

He laughed. "I enjoyed every bite of that cake. And I'm sure I'll love this one too. But I'd like to save it until I'm not so stuffed."

"Amanda and I need to have a talk with you," Grandpa said. "Mind if I close the door?"

"I have a better idea." Dwight nodded toward the window. "Since it's sunny today, I'd like to go outside. Amanda, would you be so kind as to help me get my coat and hat on?"

"Of course." I went to the closet and retrieved a brown tweed coat and a newsboy cap.

"Dave, fire up that wheelchair."

Grandpa and I got Dwight bundled into his chair, and Grandpa pushed him out into the hall. When we passed the nurse's station, I saw that the dark-haired nurse with the severe bun who'd offered to sedate Dwight after his friends died was on duty.

"Where do you think you're going?" she asked Dwight.

"I'd like to feel the sun on my face, Penelope," he answered. "I won't be long, and my friends will watch out for me."

"Okay, but don't blame me if you come down with pneumonia."

Once we got outside, Dwight pointed toward the courtyard. "Let's talk over there. The staff can see where we are but can't hear what we're saying."

We positioned Dwight in the sun, where he momentarily closed his eyes and lifted his face to bask in the warmth.

"What do you want to talk about—does it have anything to do with the box Aunt Max told me about?" he asked.

"It does." Grandpa explained that he took the box to a friend who is an appraiser. "She has the box in her safe now, but she won't try to sell the items until she hears back from me."

"Aunt Max said there was a Babe Ruth autographed card in the box." Dwight pulled his cap lower to shade his eyes. "I imagine that might be worth something."

"Monica, the appraiser, said the contents of the box are worth a minimum of two-hundred-fifty-thousand dollars."

"*Minimum?*" I gaped at Grandpa. "You didn't tell me that."

"I'm trying to be conservative and not get anyone's hopes up. After all, the items are only worth what someone is willing to pay for them."

"I don't suppose the contents of the box would be that much without the card," Dwight said. "But I'd like Zoe to have something that belonged to my dad. She never knew him, but she reminds me so much of him at times." He smiled. "You know, little things she says and does."

"You and Zoe—and Maggie also needs to be part of this decision—can discuss the contents and decide what to do." Grandpa gave Dwight a folded sheet of paper. "Here is an itemized list of the contents of the box and the value Monica has assessed each item."

Dwight scanned the list. "Huh. It's amazing that a bunch of—what some people would consider—junk could be worth so much money."

"Max wants you to use the proceeds from the sale to live a better life," I said. "I had a friend in college whose mom inherited a substantial sum of money and set up a living trust with my friend as the beneficiary."

"Do you think I could do something like that and take care of Maggie and Zoe?" He gestured toward my purse. "Have you got your phone on you?"

"Yes." I took out my phone.

"If you don't mind my borrowing it, open the calculator app and hand it here."

I gave Dwight the phone. I couldn't see what he was adding up, but he nodded with satisfaction when he handed it back a few moments later. I glanced down at the screen but saw that he'd closed the app.

"Let me talk with Maggie. If she's willing to move me in with her and Zoe, she could quit one of her jobs and take life a little easier." He folded his hands together. "Have your friend sell it all, Dave. Zoe can have the photos of my dad to keep him alive in her memory. I'll have them restored for her."

"I'm sure Max would enjoy seeing those photos as well." I paused. "Dwight, do you think there's anything odd about Max?"

"No, I think she's great." He squinted at me. "Why? Do you?"

"I love Max," I said.

"I was a little bothered by the fact that she's a ghost at first, but I got over it."

I could feel my eyes almost bug out. "You know Max is a ghost?"

"Well, sure. I'm not losing my marbles yet. At least, I don't think I am. Of course, I do talk with a ghost—but then so do you."

"And that ghost gave you a box of rare collectibles," Grandpa added.

"That's true."

"But Zoe said Aunt Max is a little secret the two of you share," I said.

"That's right—Maggie would have a conniption if she knew about Aunt Max. That's why I'll have to be careful in telling her where I got the box."

"Do you believe you'll ever be able to introduce Maggie to Max?" Grandpa asked.

"I doubt it," Dwight said. "Maggie doesn't like anything she doesn't understand."

I looked up to see Sally Jane striding across the lawn and warned the men to be quiet.

"I've come to get you, Dwight," she said. "Penelope wants you back inside. Amanda, Dave, you can walk with me if you'd like to. And I can talk with you once we get Dwight settled back in his room."

Sally Jane wheeled Dwight back into the building. Grandpa and I followed them.

In front of the nurse's station, there was a well-dressed, balding man lecturing Penelope.

"—important to potential newcomers, to families, and mainly to the Board of Directors that residents appear calm and happy."

"Hi, Mr. Godfrey," Sally Jane said.

I couldn't tell whether she was oblivious to the tension between Mr. Godfrey and Penelope or if she was simply choosing to ignore it.

Turning an icy stare in her direction, Mr. Godfrey said, "I'm in the middle of something." Then he noticed Grandpa and me. "Sorry." Although the ice didn't quite thaw, he managed a smile. "I'm Larry Godfrey, nursing home administrator. Is there anything I can help you with?"

"No, sir, we're fine." Grandpa gave him a nod. "Sally Jane, we should get Dwight back to his room."

"Indeed," Mr. Godfrey said. "Don't let me hold you up."

When we got Dwight back to his room, Sally Jane made it obvious she wasn't planning on going anywhere anytime soon. With our plans to again speak privately with Dwight thwarted, we told him goodbye and said we'd talk with him later.

"Dwight, I'll be right back, and we'll play some checkers." Sally Jane followed us into the hall and looked all around before lowering her voice. "I found out Penelope's mother is a diabetic. Do you think that might explain the missing insulin?"

"Missing insulin?" I wasn't sure what she meant.

"Yeah, the insulin missing when the nurse's dad died. It wasn't among the meds returned to the pharmacy."

Grandpa nodded. "I remember hearing about that."

"Well, it was true," Sally Jane said. "I mean, don't blame Penelope. Why should a deceased patient's medicine be thrown away instead of given to somebody else? If another patient can benefit from it, then let them have it—don't you think?"

"It would make sense," I said. "Although I'm guessing the protocols are in place for a reason."

She shrugged. "I'm just telling you what I heard. I'd better get back to Dwight."

When Grandpa and I went back down the hall toward the door, neither the hospital administrator nor Penelope were in sight.

"I'd have thought the administrator would be nicer to his volunteers," I said softly.

"True, but although he was adamant with Penelope that he wanted residents calm and happy, he appeared to be more concerned with the opinion of the Board of Directors than anything else."

We walked outside, and I turned back to make sure no one was watching us. "I wonder if the administrator could be instructing his staff to sedate residents who are rowdy or who might not present the proper image to the Board?"

Chapter Twenty-One

It was about an hour after lunch when Connie came over. After a fluttery tap on the door, she came inside the atelier carrying a bag.

"Is Jason around?" she asked.

"He might be upstairs," I said. "I'm not sure. But if you need him, I can give him a call."

She grinned. "No, I'm just making sure he's not here. I want to show you what I got him for Secret Santa."

Always eager to get into someone's business, Jazzy hopped onto the worktable when Connie opened the bag.

"You wanna see too?" Connie asked her.

"Yeah, and so do I," Max said.

I hadn't even been aware Max was around this afternoon until now. She and Jazzy were a lot alike. They always popped up when they thought something interesting was going on.

Connie removed what at first glance appeared to be a huge camera lens from the bag. I quickly realized it was a mug.

"Oh, my goodness!" I took the mug and examined it more closely. The detail was remarkable. The mug was clever as well as functional. "He's going to love this."

"You think so?" she asked.

I handed back the mug so Connie could put it back in the bag. "I know so."

"Good. I'm going to put some tea blends with it."

"You did very well," I said. "And, as far as I know, you didn't even have to hire our on-site detective."

"I didn't. But I did feel bad about being the only merchant in the building who hadn't hired her for something, so I'm paying her to research what types of essential oils people like best."

I laughed. "I'll be expecting a visit then."

"She is precocious, isn't she? Marielle has always been mature for her age, too—trying to gather knowledge everywhere she goes. Charlie is happy in his own little world." She smiled. "Kids are funny. They have their own special personalities even before they're born."

I had never met Connie's son, but her daughter shared many of her mother's personality traits. I suspected Charlie was more like Connie's husband, Will.

"Some guy just walked into Delightful Home," Max said.

"I believe you have a customer," I told Connie.

Lips parting slightly, Connie inclined her head and looked down at the floor. "I don't hear anything."

I shrugged. "I could be imagining it."

"I'd better go check," Connie said. "See you in a bit."

"Thanks for that," I told Max after Connie left. "I'd have hated for someone to steal something while she was visiting with me."

"Me too," she said. "That mug is the elephant's eyebrows, though. I didn't even know they made mugs like that."

"I didn't either, but there certainly are a lot of consumer goods available online. If you can dream it up, odds are someone has already made one."

Max took my statement as a challenge. "Are there sewing mugs? Show me on the tablet."

I went to the tablet I'd given her, unlocked it, and searched for sewing mugs. She gasped at the dozens that filled the screen.

"Fashionista mug," she said.

There were fewer mugs relating to fashionistas, but there were some.

"Toucans."

Rolling my eyes, I searched for toucan mugs. There were several. One Max and I both particularly liked had a toucan handle and the phrase "Toucan do it."

"I love it!" She clasped her hands together. "What about Constantinople? Is there a Constantinople mug?"

Believe it or not, there was.

Immediately after we searched for Constantinople mugs, Zoe requested to video chat.

"Zoe! Did you know there are Constantinople mugs?" Max asked.

"What's Constantinople?" Zoe asked.

"It's a place. And they have mugs about it," she said.

"Do you want one of these Constantinople mugs?" Zoe looked from Max to me, clearly confused as to what was going on.

"Not especially." Max flipped her palms. "You know I can't drink, but I still think it's a neat thing."

"I wanted to come to the shop today," Zoe said, "but Mom is working, and my friend can't drive me. I've already made one more hat and will finish the other one this evening. Is it all right if I come there tomorrow and work?"

"Of course, it—"

I was interrupted by a delivery guy coming in the door to reception. "Got some packages for Designs on You."

"Yes," I said, "bring them in here please."

He came on through to the atelier.

"Well, hello, good looking," Max said.

I inadvertently echoed, "Good looking."

The man looked at me with a grin. This wasn't the first time he'd heard how handsome he was, and he was expecting to hear it again. "Excuse me?"

"Good looking packages," I said. "I've been waiting for these."

"Oh, all right." He winked. "See you next time."

As the man walked back through the reception area, Zoe burst into giggles. Naturally, Max joined in.

"You two laugh it up." I opened the boxes and was relieved to see that they contained the materials for Marsha Billings' gown. "I need to cut out this pattern."

Jason came over to my house that evening for what we'd hoped would be a relaxing binge watch of all three Christmas episodes of the television series *Psych*. We had sandwiches, a veggie and fruit tray which included pineapple, and we had maple cookies. Jason had brought Rascal, so I had some treats for him to enjoy while we noshed on our snacks. Jazzy snoozed on her cat tree, not in the mood to play with the sometimes-slobbery dog.

I was snuggled up beside Jason on the sofa and put my feet on his lap. "I've decided to bring banana pudding to the potluck. Do you think that will be all right?"

"That'll be terrific. Banana pudding is one of my favorites. And Dad's too."

We'd just finished the episode, *"Gus' Dad May Have Killed an Old Guy,"* and Jason was finding the next one when I got a text.

Looking at the screen, it said the text was from me— that's how I knew it was from Max. Since I gave her my tablet, when she sends me a message, it shows up as being from myself.

It read: *Somebody slipped Dwight a Mickey Finn! He's about to go under! Get him help quick!*

I swung my feet off Jason's lap. "I have to call the nursing home."

"What's wrong?"

How could I possibly explain to Jason that my friend, the ghost, told me I have to check on Dwight immediately? I decided to defer my answer, other than to say it was about Dwight.

I called the nursing home and told the nurse who answered, "Please go check on Dwight Hall immediately. He's losing consciousness."

"How do you know?" she asked.

"We were video chatting."

"I'll go see about him," the nurse said.

"I'm on my way there," I said.

When I ended the call, Jason was frowning at me. "What's going on?"

"Sorry about the fib," I said. "Someone else was video chatting with Dwight—someone who might not have been believed if she'd called herself." The fact that Max likely wouldn't have been heard over the phone by the nurse was irrelevant.

"Ah, I see." He obviously thought the text I'd received had been from Zoe. He turned off the television. "Let's go."

We slipped on our shoes, put Rascal into Jason's SUV, and headed for the nursing home. I went onto social media and sent Max a message letting her know Jason and I were on the way.

"Do you think I should contact Maggie?" I asked Jason.

"Let's wait and see how serious the situation is," he said. "We don't want to get Zoe in trouble if it turns out to be nothing."

"Right."

When we arrived, there was an ambulance by the front entrance.

Jason let me out at the door. "Go inside and make sure Dwight is okay. I'll park and come on in."

"Thanks." I got out and ran into the building.

Before I could get to the nurse's station, I saw Dwight being wheeled out on a stretcher. There was an oxygen mask over his face.

Hurrying forward, I grasped his hand. "Dwight!"

"I need you to let him go, miss," one of the EMTs said. "We have to get him to the hospital."

"What's wrong?" I asked.

"We don't know yet."

Chapter Twenty-Two

I asked Jason to take me home to get my car, but he insisted on driving me to the hospital.

"I'll drive you there, drop you off, take Rascal home, and come back," he said.

"That's too much of an imposition," I said. "I couldn't possibly ask you to do all that."

"You aren't asking. I'm insisting. I don't really know Dwight, but I care about him too—and I'm concerned about the things going on at that nursing home."

When we got to the hospital, I hurried inside. I spotted Maggie and Zoe going into an exam room, so I followed them, rather than stopping at the nurse's station.

Inside the exam room, Dwight was asleep but hooked up to a multi-parameter monitor. The monitor was beeping rhythmically, and I decided that was a good sign.

Whether it really was, or I simply wanted it to be, was debatable.

I spoke in a hushed tone. "How is he?"

"Sleeping," Maggie answered. "We don't know anything yet."

Zoe hugged me. "The nursing home told Mom you called and made them check on him. Thank you."

"He got drowsy during a video chat," I said.

Zoe nodded. She knew Max and Dwight spoke often, so she knew what I wasn't saying in front of Maggie.

"The nurse has taken some blood and a urine sample," Maggie said. "Hopefully, they'll know something soon."

Dwight's eyes fluttered open. "H-hello? Wh-who...who's h-here?"

"It's us, Daddy—Maggie and Zoe." Maggie clutched her father's hand and stood so he could see her without lifting his head.

"Amanda is here too, Papaw," Zoe added.

"Hey, Dwight," I said. "How are you feeling?"

"S-sleepy. So sleepy." His eyes drifted closed again. "S-started when...I w-was...eating...my c-cake..."

The nurse came in. "How's our patient?"

"You tell us," Maggie said.

"He's so sleepy he can't keep his eyes open," I said. "Are you checking for sedatives in the lab work?"

"We're checking for a number of things, including sedatives." The nurse took Dwight's hand and squeezed it gently. "The good news is that his vitals are well within normal limits."

"G-good c-cake," Dwight mumbled.

Smiling, the nurse said, "He must be having pleasant dreams."

"He said he started getting sleepy when he was eating his cake," Maggie said. "I'm going to call the nursing home to see if there's any of the cake left. Maybe you could test it." She left the room.

When the nurse left, I tell Zoe Max sent me a message letting me know Dwight was in trouble. "I might've led Jason to believe you were the one chatting with your papaw."

"That's all right," she said. "I'm only glad one of us was talking with him and could save him. If there was something in that cake, it might've killed him if we hadn't gotten him here in time."

I gave her a one-armed hug. "Something in the cake…"

"What is it?" Zoe asked.

"Grandpa Dave and I went to see Dwight around lunchtime today, and I stopped at the grocery store and got your papaw a slice of coconut cake. I remembered your telling us how much he liked it."

"That was nice." Zoe frowned. "If you're worried about that, don't be. It couldn't be the same cake."

"Unless..." Unless it was. We'd left it unattended in Dwight's room when the three of us had gone outside to the courtyard.

"What cake?" Maggie asked, coming back into the room.

"The coconut cake Amanda got Papaw," Zoe answered. "That couldn't be what made him sick."

"Oh, no?" Maggie crossed her arms and glared at me. "Could I speak with you in the hall?"

We stepped into the hallway and Maggie pulled the door halfway closed. Zoe followed, staying in the doorway.

"There was a half-eaten piece of coconut cake on the table beside Daddy's laptop," she said. "Do you want to tell me what you put in that cake?"

"I didn't put anything in it," I said. "I bought it at the grocery store and never touched it."

"Mom! You know Amanda loves Papaw. She'd never do anything to hurt him."

"Well, it's pretty convenient she starts making accusations about the nursing home giving sedatives to the residents and then Dad practically passes out while eating a piece of cake *she* brought him."

I emitted a squeak of indignation. "I assure you if there was anything put in Dwight's cake, it was done after I left. Zoe is right—I'd never hurt Dwight."

Jason arrived and put his arm around me. "What's going on?"

"Dwight said he started getting sleepy while eating a piece of cake Grandpa and I took him at lunchtime," I said. "He saved the cake for later, and he asked us to take him outside to the courtyard since it was sunny. Someone must've tampered with the cake when we were out of the room."

"Yeah, that's a tidy little story," Maggie said. "Tell it to somebody who hasn't been around as long as I have. And tell it walking."

"What?" I asked.

"You heard me—get out of here. We don't need you here."

"Mom, stop! You're being a jerk!" Zoe shouted. "I was there when the nurse offered to sedate Papaw, and I know Amanda would never drug him. She loves Papaw! Maybe even more than you do—at least, she cares what happens to him in that lousy place!"

"Zoe, it's okay," I said softly. "I'll see you tomorrow."

"No, you won't," Maggie said. "My daughter's days of working in your dress shop are through."

"Mom, no!"

The nurse returned. "I'm going to have to ask you all to either keep it down or leave."

"I'm going," I said. "Please let me know if there's anything I can do."

"I think you've done enough." Maggie turned and went back into the exam room.

Zoe stood there with tears streaming down her face.

"Everything will be okay," I whispered. "Go on back inside before you get into trouble."

"I hate her," Zoe said.

"No, you don't. You're both just upset." I gave her a quick hug and then left.

As Jason and I walked down the hall, the tears I'd managed to hold at bay coursed down my cheeks.

He stopped walking and gathered me into his arms. "It's all right. Maggie is scared—she'll be better once she knows her dad will be okay."

Clinging to him, I drew in a ragged breath. "I don't understand how she could possibly think I'd do anything to hurt Dwight."

"She doesn't." He rubbed my back and kissed the top of my head. "In the morning, she'll call and apologize— wait and see."

"I'm not going to hold my breath."

It was too late to talk with Grandpa when I got home; but as I'd expected, Max was online and waiting to hear from me.

"You've been crying." Her voice was flat.

"No, it's not what you think. Dwight is fine."

"That doesn't explain your puffy eyes."

I took a deep breath. "Maggie thinks I put a sedative in the coconut cake I took Dwight. She made me leave the hospital and said Zoe can't come back to the shop again."

"Horsefeathers. Don't worry about that."

"I am worried about it. About all of it. First off, I think someone did put something in Dwight's cake. If that's the case, they had to have done it while we were outside in the courtyard because Dwight was finishing his lunch when we got there and wanted to save the cake for later."

"But it was sealed, right?" she asked. "I've seen the things you bring in here from the grocery store, and they're always sealed tighter than Dick's hatband."

"It was sealed, but there might've been a way someone could open it and then seal it back." I sighed. "I don't know. And I'm concerned that if the cake really is what the person used to drug Dwight, what would have happened if he'd eaten the entire thing?"

"No." She wagged a finger at me. "Don't do that. Never concern yourself with what could've happened. It didn't. Learn from it and move forward."

"But we can't even learn from it," I said. "Maggie thinks I did it, and she's not even looking in the right direction."

"Dwight will set her straight."

"Are you sure? Because I'm not. What if he also thinks I did it?"

"Why would he think that?" she asked.

"Maybe he'd get it into his head that I'd do it so Grandpa and I could keep the proceeds from the sale of your Dad's strongbox."

"Oh, that's not a bad idea." She rested her chin on her palm. "I'm glad Maggie doesn't know about the box yet, because that does give you one heck of a motive to slip Dwight a Mickey Finn."

"Who is Mickey Finn?" I asked.

"I don't know. Somebody who used to drug people without their knowledge, I imagine. I'm guessing that's where the saying came from." She frowned. "Back to the important stuff—who would've drugged Dwight and why?"

"I can come up with only one reason—whoever killed the other residents is anxious because we're poking around in their business," I said. "I believe they hoped this would warn us away from asking any more questions."

"I don't know." She drummed her fingers against her cheek. "Maybe. Or it could be for the reason the others were killed."

"Which is?"

"I haven't got that figured out yet," she said. "But that's something we need to do—quick."

"I know. But it's going to be hard now that Zoe is banned from seeing me." I fought back tears. "Maggie might even have me banned from the nursing home now too."

"One problem at a time, darling. Go get some sleep and we'll ruminate together later."

As I got ready for bed, I found myself wondering what all the residents who died had in common.

Chapter Twenty-Three

When Jazzy and I got to work on Thursday morning, Max wasn't there. I guessed she'd expended too much of her energy last night.

After I got Jazzy settled and cleaned off the worktable to start cutting out Marsha Billings' dress, Grandpa came by.

"Hi." I stopped what I was doing to give him a hug. "What are you doing here?"

"I got a message from Max telling me what happened last night."

I slumped into one of the sewing machine chairs. "I feel so stupid. Why did I take that cake to Dwight in the first place?"

"You did it because you're thoughtful." He sat in another of the chairs and rolled closer to me. "You can't beat yourself up because someone saw your act of kindness as an opportunity to frame you or to shift blame."

"We have to find out what each of the deceased residents had in common—other than being unruly and then presumably being sedated. There has to be more to their deaths than that—and I don't think their deaths are coincidental." I shuddered. "Dwight might've eaten that entire slice of cake and died had he not been talking with Max at the time."

"She told me you'd say that, and she said to remind you she warned you not to dwell on what could've happened," Grandpa said. "Because of you, Dwight is fine."

After briefly tapping on the door, Jason came into the workroom and closed the door behind him. Not that it mattered much, since Jazzy had already hopped up onto Grandpa's lap, but I'm glad he was being mindful of her.

He came over and hugged me. "Are you all right this morning?"

I waffled my hand. "I hate that Maggie thinks I put something in her dad's cake."

Jason shook his head. "Like I told you last night, when she can think rationally again, she'll know better."

Grandpa and I exchanged a look—he was the first to look away. He wasn't any more convinced than I was that Maggie Flannagan wouldn't continue to believe I'd drugged her dad until her dying day.

"The fact remains that someone did drug Dwight," Jason said, "which makes me wonder what that person had in store for him."

"I've been thinking the same thing," I said. "Had Dwight eaten that entire piece of cake, his fate could've been the same as those who died."

"Yeah, it's a really good thing he was video chatting with Zoe when he started acting strange." Jason shook his head. "And thank goodness, she thought to call you. Although I have to admit, I think it's sad she didn't run and get her mother right away."

Neither Grandpa nor I weighed in on that statement. I mean, short of correcting Jason and telling him Dwight wasn't talking with Zoe but with his dead aunt, what could we say?

"We have to consider the possibility that whoever drugged Dwight might strike out at him again," Grandpa said.

"And even if it isn't Dwight, that person is sure to target someone else, if it's the same one who drugged the other residents," I said. "Grandpa and I have been trying to determine what the deceased residents had in common."

Grandpa stroked Jazzy's head. "Since the one man's insulin disappeared, I'm wondering if someone is stealing residents' medication."

"That's possible," Jason said. "I'll ask Ryan to look into it—see if any of the recently deceased patients had any illnesses in common or if any of their medication was reported missing at or prior to their deaths."

"Would you please also ask Ryan if he can determine for certain that the drug that knocked Dwight out was found in the cake?" I asked. "And maybe he could also tell us what it is. Anyone could dose a resident with an over-the-counter sleep aid or allergy medication, but—presumably—only a medical professional would have access to a prescription medication."

"All right." Jason nodded. "I need to go upstairs, get my equipment, and leave, but I'll call Ryan on the drive to my appointment." He kissed my cheek, shook Grandpa's hand, and patted Jazzy's head.

Was that guy a keeper, or what?

Jason left the shop, and we heard his tread on the stairs.

"Before I leave, why don't we call the nursing home and check on Dwight?" Grandpa suggested.

I got out my phone, called the nursing home, and put the phone on speaker.

"Good morning. This is Winter Garden Nursing Home. How may I help you today?"

"Hi, this is Amanda Tucker. My grandfather and I are calling to check on Dwight Hall. He had to be—"

"One moment while I transfer you to our administrator."

I arched a brow at Grandpa, and he shrugged.

"Larry Godfrey, how may I help you?"

"Good morning, Mr. Godfrey," I said. "My grandfather and I are calling to check on Dwight Hall, and your receptionist put us through to you."

"Yes...well...I'm sorry to tell you that Maggie Flannagan has asked that neither you nor your grandfather have any further contact with her father," Mr. Godfrey said.

"Can you just tell me how Dwight is doing this morning?" I asked. "Is he back from the hospital yet?"

"I can't release any information to you about Mr. Hall. Again, I apologize, Ms. Tucker, but since a family member has requested the ban, I must enforce it. Goodbye." He ended the call.

I turned to Grandpa incredulously. "He can't even tell us Dwight is okay? Or whether or not he's there? What's up with that?" I had another thought. "And what are we supposed to do about the box?"

"I don't know, Pup. Based on what Dwight told me, I told Monica to sell it all yesterday. She has already put the items on an auction site."

Following three sharp raps on the door, Trish Oakes strolled into the room. "I'm sorry to interrupt, but I saw your truck outside, Mr. Tucker, and I wanted to say hello."

"Thank you," he said. "That's awfully kind of you."

"How is your friend? The one who was interested in the space?" she asked. "Do you think he'd like to come see the place today?"

"She might," Grandpa said. "I'll check with her."

"*She*?" Ms. Oakes frowned. "I thought your friend was a gentleman who was interested in opening a hobby shop...you know, with all the outlets?"

"Different friend." He grinned. "This one would be much easier to get along with, I imagine."

"Well, I wouldn't turn either of them away if they met our requirements," she said.

"I need to be running along." He kissed my cheek. "Get back to work, young lady, and I'll talk with you in a little while."

"All right," I said.

"I'll walk you out." Ms. Oakes linked her arm through his, leaving me to wonder if she was interested in my grandpa romantically or if she just really wanted to lease that space.

I hoped she was simply desperate to rent out the shop upstairs.

Not quite ready to get back to Marsha Billings' dress, I opened my laptop and logged into my social media account. I had a message notification and opened it eagerly. Maybe it was Zoe.

It wasn't from Zoe. It was from Krista, Ms. Oakes' daughter.

She wrote: *Hi, Amanda. Thank you for reaching out to me! I have to admit, I'm surprised and delighted to learn Mom has friends like you at Shops on Main. She led me to believe she didn't have any friends at work whatsoever. I would love to come visit her either during Christmas or the week after. Whatever you can work out would be great with me. I am so grateful and appreciative you're doing this for us! XOXO, Krista*

Well, I'd be buying a plane ticket for Krista for Ms. Oakes' Secret Santa present. I wondered if anyone, other than Connie, would agree to pitch in on the cost. If not, it would be okay. I'd put it on my credit card and pay it off as soon as I could. That's the kind of stuff *friends like me* do. I felt a stab of guilt. I needed to be a better friend to Ms. Oakes. But how could you be a friend to someone who didn't seem to want one?

Chapter Twenty-Four

Seeing that Jazzy was napping on her bed, I went next door to visit Connie. I browsed while she finished up with a customer.

When the lady left, Connie joined me in front of the essential oils display. "Here to shop or to talk?"

"Talk, at the moment." I told her about Krista's message. "I replied asking her if she was free to talk later today, and I gave her my number." I sighed. "I feel horrible about her comment that she didn't think her mom had any work friends. *You're* her friend, aren't you?"

"Eh." Connie grimaced. "I wouldn't say we're friends like you and I are. When Trish took over as building manager, Melba Meacham told her I'd been here the longest and to come to me with any questions she might have. She didn't have many, but she did come to me to get the lowdown on the other merchants."

I didn't dare ask about the lowdown on me. "I'm hesitant to ask anyone else about helping pay for Krista's ticket home."

"Don't be," Connie said. "Simply tell everyone what you're doing and ask if they'd like to contribute. If not, it's no big deal."

"I'm also going to get something to wrap for Ms. Oakes as well—maybe a 'home for the holidays' ornament." I smiled. "Whether the others contribute or not, I'm excited about bringing Krista home for a visit. It would be nice, though, if we could say her visit is a gift from all of us because it would show her that we all do care about her mother."

"Well, don't forget, I told you when you came up with the idea that I'm in."

"Thanks, Connie. Now to figure out how to bring up the subject to the other merchants without Ms. Oakes finding out what I'm up to."

"Let me think on that for a little bit." She adjusted some bottles on the shelf. "I'll be over to chat when I have an idea."

When I returned to Designs on You, Max was sitting on my desk swinging her legs. "That old battle axe could have a lot of friends if she'd be nice to people. Would her face crack if she'd smile?"

"It didn't this morning when she smiled at Grandpa."

"Nah, that didn't count. I'm guessing it wasn't a sincere smile—that was a smile of desperation. Insincere smiles don't fool anyone. Me, in particular."

"Have you heard from Zoe?" I asked.

"No, but I'm not worried. Who knows when the kid got to sleep last night…or this morning? I'd imagine she's still nestled under her covers." She gave me a wistful grin. "I used to adore snuggling under mine. I always had a big pile of blankets over me. It's funny the things you miss."

Max had disappeared for some rest and I was cutting out Marsha Billings' dress when Grandpa brought an attractive, auburn-haired, sixty-something woman into the shop.

"Hi, Pup," he said, as he closed the door behind them. "This is Monica Miller, my appraiser friend."

Monica was well dressed in navy slacks, a white sweater, and a navy-print scarf. She looked at some of the garments I had hanging in the workroom but was careful not to touch them.

"Monica, it's a pleasure to meet you," I said. "Would you like to go into the main area and see the clothes?"

"I'd love to."

As I led Monica into the retail portion of the shop, I wondered why Grandpa had brought her here. Even though we were in hot water with Maggie, I knew the auction was still going forward on Dwight's behalf. Was Monica here to talk with Grandpa and me about the contents of the strongbox?

Monica immediately went to a dress I had on the mannequin. It was a bias-cut, 1930s-style black satin dress with puff sleeves.

She let out a low whistle. "This is incredible. After I make my commission on the collectibles I'm selling for Mr. Hall, I'm going to have to buy this gown."

"So...um...how is that going?" I ventured a glance at Grandpa, who was playing with Jazzy and not paying any attention to me. I couldn't tell if his distraction was contrived or not.

"It's going well," Monica said. "May I try this on?"

"Of course. That dress is from the ready-to-wear line, so it's available in several sizes. If you'll come right this way, we can get one in your size."

"Fantastic." Monica encompassed Grandpa and me in her smile, but Grandpa was still absorbed with Jazzy.

Not that he didn't love the cat, but I had the distinct feeling he was faking going overboard with the playtime. What wasn't he telling me? While Monica was trying on the dress, I intended to find out.

"What's going on with you?" I whispered to him.

"Just playing with little Jasmine here."

I tightened my lips and widened my eyes. "Grandpa…"

"Fine." He lowered his voice. "I kind of like Monica."

"I thought that was obvious. If you didn't like her, you wouldn't have trusted Max's collectibles to her."

"I mean, since I've been spending a little time with her, I'm thinking I might *like* like her. But I don't want to blow it by asking her out and then maybe not liking her as much as I'd hoped when I might be seeing her more often."

"Might be seeing her more often?"

Before I could get clarification on that, Monica came out in the black dress. She looked fabulous.

"Wow." Grandpa said the word under his breath, but she heard him. And she liked that he'd noticed.

"You think it would be a good investment then, Dave?" she asked.

"I believe it would be an excellent investment."

She laughed. "Then why wait for a commission? I'll take it now. Let me go get changed, and we'll head on upstairs."

"Upstairs?" I echoed.

"Yes. Didn't Dave tell you? I'm here to look at the vacant space," she said. "I have quite a few collectibles of my own, and I'd like to have a more formal setup for meeting with clients than what I have now—meeting them in a quiet corner of the public library."

"Now I see what you're talking about," I said, softly, as Monica went to change out of the dress. "For what it's worth, I like her."

"Me, too," he said. "But I need to tread carefully if she ends up renting space in your building."

When Monica and Grandpa went upstairs to speak with Ms. Oakes, I put the dress in a garment bag.

Max appeared on the filing cabinet with a scowl on her face. "Who was Ms. Hoity-Toity?"

"I imagine you already know she's the appraiser who's selling your dad's collectibles at auction, and her name is Monica Miller." Max sometimes eavesdropped before she popped in.

"Yeah, I know. I'm not as sold on her as you seem to be."

"I'm not sold on her—and neither is Grandpa," I said. "But I'd rather Grandpa date her than Ms. Oakes."

"I thought you were being all nicey-nicey with old Sour Puss now."

"That doesn't mean I want the woman dating my grandpa." I hung up the garment bag. "Besides, no matter who Grandpa dates, he'll never stop caring for you."

"I know. It's not that—you folks are family to me, and I want you both to be happy. It's just sometimes I miss things, you know? Like burying myself under covers and feeling the silky material of a new dress against my skin...having a taste of sweet tea or chocolate..." She shrugged. "It's no big deal. But always remember to treasure the little things."

It was almost lunchtime when I got a call from an unknown number. I always answer, thinking the caller might be someone who has my business card or who got my number from a friend.

"Hello, Designs on You, Amanda speaking. How may I help you?"

"It's me, Zoe. I'm calling from a friend's phone because Mom is monitoring mine to make sure I don't talk with you or Dave."

"I'm so sorry for all of this," I said.

"It's not fair. I know you didn't drug Papaw. But you're being treated like a criminal, and I am too."

"Hang in there," Max said over my shoulder. "I got in plenty of trouble with your grouchy old great-great-grandmother in my day, but everything always worked itself out. Maggie will be over her mad spell in a day or two."

"I don't know," Zoe said. "She's really upset. She thinks Amanda put sleeping medicine in Papaw's cake to prove she was right about patients being sedated, but I know that's a load of hooey—I mean, garbage."

Max's slang really was rubbing off on Zoe.

"But how can I convince her of that?" Zoe asked.

"It would go a long way in mending fences if we could find out who really did drug him," Max said. "Does he remember anything about that day?"

"Specifically, after Grandpa and I left," I added.

"I'll ask him when the warden gives me the chance. I'd better run before she catches me."

I was sorry Maggie was keeping such close tabs on Zoe. How could she believe I'd actually drug her dad?

"We'll talk to you when we can," I said. But Zoe had already ended the call.

Blowing out a breath, I looked at Max. "Now what?"

"Prayer would be a good start."

Chapter Twenty-Five

While I worked on Marsha Billings' dress, Max video chatted with Dwight. He was angry that Maggie had ordered Grandpa and me banned from the nursing home.

"They're *my* friends, and they can come see me if I want them to!" he shouted.

"Shhh!" Max put a finger to her lips. "Be quiet, or somebody might come in there and give you a sedative."

"Oh…right. It just makes my blood boil, that's all." He leaned forward and peered into his camera.

I could tell he wanted to address me, so I put down my scissors and stepped closer to Max. "Hi, Dwight."

"Hi, honey. I want you and Dave to come see me this afternoon," he said. "Can you do that?"

"We don't want to cause trouble for you," I said. "Our coming to the nursing home will not only get you in trouble with the staff but with Maggie too."

"I don't care. My daughter needs to stop treating me like I'm helpless, and pretty soon, I'll have the money to leave here—God willing—so I don't care what they say either."

"But, Dwight, we have to keep you safe until you *can* leave the nursing home," I said.

"I agree with Amanda, darling," Max said. "And you know how I'm usually the first person eager to rock the boat."

"You've both lost your nerve." He raised his chin, making it obvious he was issuing a challenge.

I looked at Max, and she shrugged.

"You and Dave come see me this afternoon," Dwight said. "Let me know when you're on your way, and I'll meet you at the front door. If they try to throw you out, they'll have to toss me out as well. You're my guests, and I want you there."

The thought of having a showdown with the nursing home administrator because Maggie had convinced him I'd drugged Dwight made me feel queasy. But I knew I had to do whatever was necessary to get back into the nursing home and find out who put the antihistamine—or whatever was used to sedate Dwight—in his cake. Not only did that person send Dwight to the hospital, but they framed me. Was the cake simply the most convenient way of administering the drug, or was making me look guilty intentional?

I heard the door to the reception room open. "Excuse me. You guys be quiet for a minute okay?"

I hurried into the reception room, closing the door to the workroom behind me and praying Max and Dwight—well, Dwight, anyway—wouldn't say anything while I was gone.

Connie had come into the reception area and was standing by the window.

"Hi, there." I smiled. "Is it bad that I'm relieved you're not a client?"

She laughed. "Not at all. I feel that way too on busy days."

"Things have been crazy lately."

"I understand," she said. "But I've come up with an idea about hitting the merchants up for money to help pay for Krista's ticket. Print out a note setting forth the situation—what you learned from Sienna, what Krista told you in her message, yadda, yadda—and explain that you're buying a plane ticket to bring Krista home for Christmas."

"Actually, I've already booked the ticket. Krista is scheduled to arrive on Sunday before the Secret Santa party."

"Excellent." She clasped her hands, making her bangle bracelets jingle. "Include that in the note and tell them you're doing this as your Secret Santa gift to Trish. Reveal the cost of the ticket and say you plan to tell Trish the gift of her daughter's homecoming is from all of us. If anyone would like to contribute toward the cost of the ticket, that would be wonderful but isn't necessary. I believe that making the gift from everyone will make them feel compelled to give a little something, don't you?"

"I guess." First the nursing home, and now the merchants. Ugh.

"Also, including some sort of small treat with the request couldn't hurt," she said.

"Right. That's a wonderful idea," I said. "I'll get the notes printed out before I leave today."

"Glad I could help!" Connie left to go back to her shop.

I looked over to see Max's head poking through the wall between the two rooms. "I'd have never guessed Connie to be such a manipulative little minx. I like it."

Later that afternoon, I called Grandpa.

"Hey, Pup. How's your day?"

"Well, it's shaping up to be filled with strife and schemes," I said. "How's yours?"

"I'm not in it with you. What's going on over there? Do I need to come kick somebody's butt?"

Chuckling, I replied, "No, but hold that thought." I laid out for him Dwight's plan to have us show up at the nursing home later today. "What do you think?"

"It feels a little soon for us to be pressing our luck," he said.

"I agree. On the other hand, I'll never be able to clear my name and find out who drugged Dwight unless we get back in the nursing home. And while Dwight is there and we're not, he's vulnerable to another attack."

"I agree." He blew out a breath. "We might as well go. What have we got to lose?"

"There's the possibility one of us might gain a houseguest. What if the nursing home kicks Dwight out?"

"They won't," Grandpa said. "They're making too much money off him to do that."

I closed up shop at the end of the day and took Jazzy to Grandpa's house. We fed her and left her there while we visited the nursing home.

Grandpa parked the truck near the front entrance. "Are you ready?"

"No, but we might as well go and get this over with."

We got out of the truck, and I made a conscious effort to hold up my head and straighten my back. I was as ready as I'd ever be.

Entering the nursing home, the first person we saw was Dwight. His face broke into a wide grin. Other residents were sitting near the large Christmas tree located in the center of the lobby.

Before we could get to Dwight, Mr. Godfrey barreled out of his office. "Ms. Tucker, I told you on the phone earlier today that you are banned from this establishment."

"I beg your pardon!" Dwight's voice boomed, closing the distance between us before he could physically get to us. "Amanda and Dave are my guests. If you ban them, then I'm leaving too."

"Mr. Hall, I'm afraid you don't understand—" Mr. Godfrey began.

"I understand everything. There's not a doggone thing wrong with my mind. That's why I'm the person who decides who comes here to visit me and who doesn't."

Penelope came around from behind the desk to place a hand on Dwight's shoulder. "But, Dwight, we believe Ms. Tucker put a sedative into the cake she brought you."

"You might believe that malarky, but I don't. Have these accusations against Amanda been proven?" he asked.

I wished Max was seeing this—she'd be so proud of her nephew!

"No, but—" Penelope broke off, shooting a helpless glance at Mr. Godfrey.

"Then she, Dave, and I are going to my room to enjoy a visit," Dwight said. "Do either of you have a problem with that?"

Mr. Godfrey shook his head. "No." He glared at me. "But we will keep a close eye on you."

"Good," I said. "Thank you."

The three of us headed for Dwight's room.

I took his arm and gave it a squeeze. When we were out of earshot of Penelope and Mr. Godfrey, I said softly, "You were fantastic."

"I was pretty good, wasn't I?"

"Magnificent," Grandpa said.

"Psst, Amanda!"

I turned to see Sally Jane standing in the hallway adjacent to the one leading to Dwight's room. "Hi, Sally Jane. I didn't think you were here on Thursdays."

"I'm usually not," she said.

"Pup, we're going on to Dwight's room and will see you there," Grandpa said.

"Okay." I walked closer to Sally Jane. "Is everything okay?"

"Yeah, I dropped in today to see how Dwight is doing. I'm glad to see you and your grandpa here. The last I heard, Dwight's daughter was having a fit and wanting Godfrey to keep you out of this place."

I inclined my head. "There was some tension."

"Well, anyway, I'm glad it worked out." She took an inhaler from her purse and used it.

"I didn't know you had asthma."

Shrugging, she said, "It's not bad, but I sometimes have a hard time breathing when I'm stressed. Holidays and all, you know." She dropped the inhaler back into her purse. "When I'm here visiting with the residents, I have to put my purse in the medicine closet—all the nurses do that too—to make sure none of the residents get into anything they shouldn't."

I caught a movement from the corner of my eye and turned. Penelope was watching us from the lobby. "I should go. Thank you for looking out for Dwight, Sally Jane."

"You're welcome. Glad to be of help."

Chapter Twenty-Six

D wight and Grandpa were playing checkers when I stepped into Dwight's room. The board was set up in an odd configuration, and I frowned.

Grandpa shook his head slightly, and I realized they weren't really playing checkers.

"Babe Ruth," Dwight said.

Grandpa stacked two black checkers in one square and then placed single red checkers in the five squares to the right of the black ones.

Were they using the game to communicate the current auction bids for the strongbox collectibles? And, if so, was the Babe Ruth autographed card currently at two-hundred-thousand dollars?

I knew the auctions were scheduled to run for a week and that Monica expected the bids to increase significantly near the end of the auctions. But if that one item—granted, the most valuable item—was already at two-hundred-thousand dollars, how much more would the collectibles bring?

If anyone knew about the strongbox, they'd have no problem thinking I might have slipped Dwight a Mickey Finn, as Max put it. I felt certain people had been knocked out—and worse—for a lot less.

When we got back to Grandpa's house, we made spaghetti.

Still flabbergasted by the amount of money already bid on the collectibles, I asked, "Did you speak to Dwight before I got into the room about leaving the nursing home? With the kind of money he'll be getting, he could do almost anything he wanted."

"I mentioned that, but Dwight is of the opinion that the money earned from the sale of the collectibles isn't real until the auctions are over and the money is in his account or a trust or whatever he decides to do with it," Grandpa said. "And he's right."

"But Dwight isn't safe there. He needs to leave." I put the pasta in the boiling water. "Last night is proof of that."

"I realize that, Pup." He pre-heated the oven for the frozen meatballs. "But Dwight is being extra careful right now."

"I know, but I'm still worried. And Max is too."

He shrugged. "Unfortunately, there's not much we can do, and Dwight won't act until he knows that money is a done deal."

My cell phone rang, and I took it from my pocket to look at the screen. It was Deputy Hall. I answered and put him on speaker.

"Hi, Deputy Hall."

"Hey, Amanda. Please call me Ryan. I wanted to let you know I went to see Cousin Dwight earlier today while I was still in uniform. Jason told me what happened last night, and I thought letting the nursing home staff see that Dwight has a family member who can and will arrest them might be beneficial."

"Good thinking," I said.

"Also, there is a common thread among the recently-deceased residents of the nursing home—they all had Type 2 diabetes and were taking insulin."

"But Dwight isn't diabetic."

"Right," Ryan said. "I think maybe the killer felt you were getting too close to the truth and needed to get either you or Dwight out of the way. That's why the sedative was put into the cake you brought."

"So, you do believe the residents were murdered? That their deaths weren't coincidental?" I asked.

"My beliefs are irrelevant until I can prove it, but yes, there's definitely something shady going on at that nursing home."

"Hello, deputy. Dave Tucker here with Amanda. Regarding the woman whose dad's insulin was missing, could the killer be eliminating residents in order to steal their insulin? Maybe the murderer is diabetic and needs the medication."

"I checked on that, sir. He was the only patient whose insulin was reported missing."

"Then there has to be another connection," I said. "There has to be something we're not seeing yet."

"I'll keep digging," Ryan said.

"So will we."

He groaned. "I'll pretend I didn't hear that."

On Friday morning, I drove to the Down South Café and bought a box of doughnuts before going to work. I was still the first person there, so I slipped the notes under everyone's door except for Connie's and Ms. Oakes', of course. I added the note, "Fresh doughnuts in the kitchen."

Frank and Ella were the first to respond. When they entered the shop through the workroom door, Frank had a cup of coffee in one hand and a doughnut in the other.

"What an angel!" Frank said. "Fresh doughnuts and a pot of coffee. We should make this an every-Friday occurrence."

I laughed. "I'm glad you're enjoying them."

Ella handed me a sealed envelope. "It's not much, but it's all we can do right now, what with it being so close to Christmas, the grandkids coming to visit, and all."

"Of course. Thank you for contributing—everything helps, and I merely wanted to be able to tell Ms. Oakes we all pitched in to give her such a nice surprise. It really bothered me that her daughter didn't think she had any work friends."

"Well, she doesn't," Ella said. "Even though we're all technically our own bosses, as the building manager, she's in a supervisory role. It's hard to be friends with a boss." She lifted her thin shoulders. "Still, as a mother myself, I can't stand the thought of Ms. Oakes and her daughter being apart, especially at this time of the year."

Frank nodded, his mouth full of doughnut. Finally, he swallowed and said, "Ella was miffed over this Secret Santa thing at first because we had to dip into the pot twice—Ms. Oakes had us both draw names, not draw as a couple. But my girl here has a bigger heart than she wants people to know."

Ella frowned at him and flicked him on the arm. "Oh, hush and eat your doughnut."

"Thank you both again," I said.

Ford and Sienna also popped in and gave me an envelope, and then Jason came downstairs and asked me how much I needed. I told him I didn't need anything but that if he wanted to contribute, he was welcome to do so.

I was relieved that asking the other merchants to chip in hadn't been such a big deal. Besides, wouldn't it be a good thing for all of us if our building manager was in a happier mood?

By lunchtime I was concerned because I hadn't seen Max yet. I muttered for the umpteenth time, "Max, I hope you're all right."

She materialized—barely—to tell me, "I stayed with Dwight over video chat until the wee hours of the morning. I was too worried about him not to be there. Everything was fine, and he tried to get me to leave, but I wouldn't." She smiled slightly. "I think I sang him to sleep singing *Bury Me Beneath the Willow*. Dot and I used to listen to that all the time after the Carter Family recorded it at Bristol Sessions."

"Have you heard from Zoe?" I asked.

Shaking her head, she said, "No, but Dwight told me she was coming to the nursing home to spend the day with him."

She had no more than gotten out the words than she disappeared again. But at least I knew she was all right. I went to the laptop and reached out to Dwight and Zoe on social media.

"Hey, Amanda!" Zoe seemed delighted to hear from me. "What are you working on today?"

"I'm almost finished with Marsha Billings' dress."

"I'd love to see it," she said. "But I'm glad Papaw blessed out Mr. Godfrey and made it to where you and Dave can come see him again."

"You should have seen him," I told her, as Dwight plastered a smug grin on his face. "He was something else."

"That's what he said." She grinned. "Is Max there?"

"No. She's pooped and needed to rest for a while."

"No wonder." Dwight chuckled. "She designated herself my guardian angel last night and wouldn't leave until she started fading out. I have to say, I'm glad I've been able to get to know the woman I heard so many stories about growing up. I'd have never thought that would be possible this side of heaven."

"I won't keep you," I said. "You two have fun together and call me if you need anything."

"Will do," Zoe said. "I wish Papaw could live with Mom and me and get out of this stupid place."

I looked at Dwight but didn't dare comment.

"Maybe I can sometime soon," Dwight said. "We never know what life has in store for us."

I was surprised when Sally Jane came into Designs on You that afternoon. She was timid and seemed to be overwhelmed as she walked around the shop.

"You have so many beautiful things in here," she said, reverently touching the sleeve of a dress in the ready-to-wear line.

"Would you like to try that on?"

"No." She backed away as if she'd seen a spider on the garment. "Everything in here is way out of my price range. I only came by to show you something." She took a bottle of over-the-counter allergy medication out of her coat pocket. "This fell out of Penelope's purse this morning."

I took the pill bottle and read the label.

"Although I'm not scheduled to be at the nursing home on Fridays, I promised you I'd help keep an eye on

Dwight," she said. "And I keep my promises. His granddaughter was with him when I was there, and he seemed fine."

"How did you get these pills without Penelope noticing?" I asked.

"Oh, she spilled her purse, and stuff went everywhere." She rolled her eyes. "It was chaos scrambling to pick up everything before one of the residents got hold of something. Anyway, I slipped these into my pocket when Penelope wasn't looking."

I handed the bottle back to her.

"I'd never outright accuse Penelope of anything," Sally Jane continued, "but I happened to think she might've used these pills to knock out Dwight. Did I do the right thing in bringing them to you? Should I have given them to that handsome policeman who's kin to Dwight instead?"

"No, you did the right thing," I said. "Hang onto the pills, and I'll get in touch with Deputy Hall and let him know what you've discovered. Merely finding the pills doesn't mean anything—it could be that Penelope suffers from allergies."

It was possible but given everything else happening at the nursing home and Penelope's willingness—even eagerness—to sedate residents made me feel it was doubtful. Still, a bottle of allergy pills anyone could buy at any local pharmacy was hardly the smoking gun we needed.

After Sally Jane left, I called Ryan and left him a message asking that he consider looking into Penelope's background.

Chapter Twenty-Seven

Grandpa came over on Friday evening to help me make the banana pudding I was taking to Jason's potluck after work tomorrow afternoon.

After pre-heating the oven, I got out a saucepan. "I thought that if you want to get started on the actual pudding, I'll cut up the bananas and start layering them and the vanilla wafers in the casserole dish."

"You got it, Pup." He raised his eyebrows. "You're not going to learn a lot over there at the kitchen table, though."

"I'll work at the counter so I can see what you're doing." I moved my bananas, box of wafers, and casserole dish to the counter.

Grandpa measured a cup of packed brown sugar into the saucepan. "I haven't made banana pudding in ages."

"I know, and you make the absolute best." I placed the slices of banana in the bottom of the casserole dish. "Thank you for doing this."

"Why, you're welcome. I'm glad to do it."

"I know. I love spending time with you. I hope Dwight gets to move in with Maggie and Zoe." I rested my head against his shoulder for a second. "It would be great for them—at least, it would for Dwight and Zoe."

I'd always had Grandpa nearby, and I adored him. I couldn't imagine life without him. I shook off the thought and put a layer of vanilla wafers atop my bananas.

As I continued filling the dish with banana slices and wafers, I thought about Grandma Jodie and how she'd have been singing—loudly and offkey—had she been bustling around the kitchen with us. Mom would have told me something was wrong with how I was filling the casserole dish and would have taken over, not because I was really doing it wrong but because she enjoyed doing it herself. Dad would've been eating the vanilla wafers faster than I could get them into the dish.

"You're awfully quiet," Grandpa said. "What's on your mind?"

"People who aren't here." I took a deep breath and started belting out *Shine On, Harvest Moon*.

He laughed. "I miss her too, Pup. I miss her too—horrible singing and all."

Early Saturday morning, Ms. Oakes came sailing into Designs on You with Monica Miller in tow.

"Good morning, Amanda. I'd like you to meet our newest merchant—oh, wait." She put her hand to her chest and giggled. "Silly me, what am I talking about? You two already know each other."

"Hi, Amanda," Monica said. "I don't know you as well as I'd like, but I look forward to getting acquainted with everyone here."

"It'll be nice getting to know you better too," I said.

"Monica, I'm terribly sorry you didn't arrive in time to participate in the Secret Santa gift exchange," Ms. Oakes said. "But I hope you'll still join us for our party tomorrow."

"I have plans; but if they fall through, I'll take you up on that generous offer—thanks."

"Hello, hello!" Marsha Billings breezed into the reception area as if someone had arrived ahead of her heralding her arrival.

Thankfully, she closed the door behind her. Not only did that keep Jazzy inside, it gave me the opportunity to go ahead and make the proclamation she seemed to desire.

"Monica, Ms. Oakes, I'd like you to meet Marsha Billings," I said.

Both women said it was nice to meet her, and Ms. Oakes jumped in to tell Marsha that Monica was getting ready to open an absolutely charming establishment upstairs and that she must stop in to admire it after the first of the year.

"I'll do that," Marsha said. "But right now, I'm here for my Lady Mary gown. Wait until you get a load of *that* if you want to see something charming."

I got the dress for her and she went into the changing area to put it on. Between Marsha and Ms. Oakes, I was getting an overload of exuberance this morning. When I glanced at Monica and saw that she was pressing her lips together to suppress her laughter, I knew we were going to get along fine.

Marsha sashayed out of the changing area as if she were getting ready to go into the Downton Abbey dining room to sit among her suitors. She did a turn and gave us a coquettish look over her shoulder. "Isn't it extraordinary? I adore it!"

"It certainly is gorgeous," Monica said.

"It's made me breathless." Marsha walked over to her purse, removed an inhaler, and administered a dose of albuterol. "Whew! I can't be breathless—I'm singing at an event this afternoon."

"Is it challenging for you to sing when you're asthmatic?" Ms. Oakes asked.

"Oh, I'm not." Marsha put the inhaler back into her purse before admiring herself in the mirror. "I've had a cold, so I picked up the inhaler at the drugstore to help open up my airways." After one more appreciative glance, she said, "I'd better get changed. Amanda, dear, you have done even better than I'd hoped. I look even more beautiful than Lady Mary."

"Indeed, you do," I told her. I remembered she'd initially told me she wanted the dress because the other women made her feel inferior. I had trouble believing that now.

"Someone needs a confidence boost," Ms. Oakes muttered under her breath when Marsha went to change.

"Definitely." I grinned.

When Marsha came out, I bagged up her dress, she paid for it, and left, instructing us, "Look for me online! You can hear samples of my music there. It could be a beautiful, special gift to share with your loved ones."

Marsha left and we saw her sashaying down the sidewalk.

"I need to be off as well," Monica said. "Look for me upstairs after New Year's Day! You can buy collectibles there. You might find a beautiful, special gift to share with your loved ones."

Ms. Oakes and I tittered. I thought maybe that was the first time I'd ever heard Ms. Oakes laugh.

I went to get a cup of coffee and saw Ford in the kitchen. "Good morning. Will Sienna be at the Secret Santa party tomorrow?"

A pained expression briefly crossed his face. "I've been with her all week. I was looking forward to having the entire weekend off."

"Oh, but Ford, it's a party. I mean, if she can't be here, I understand, but I'm going shopping tonight and wanted to get her a little something."

"I'll see what I can do."

I heard footsteps in the hallway before Jason leaned against the doorframe. "Morning."

Ford and I both greeted him.

"Amanda, can I see you for a moment?" Jason asked.

Wagging his head like a dog figurine on a dashboard, Ford said, "Somebody wants kisses." He made kissing faces at us before he left the kitchen.

I wrinkled my nose at Jason. "Sorry about that."

"Why? I don't care." He stepped into the room, and I saw he carried a wrapped package. "And I *do* want kisses." He gave me a quick peck on the lips.

After I'd gotten my coffee, we went into the workroom.

"What's that?" I asked.

"It's a gift I got you to let you know how much I care about and support you."

I took the package he handed me, and it was heavier than I'd expected it to be. "You're not expecting this meeting to go well, are you?"

"Of course, I am." He nodded toward the gift. "Open it."

I opened it to find a thick, hardcover book on fashion. It contained illustrations and quotes from all the top designers.

"Jason, I love it!"

"I'm glad." He drew me to him for a more thorough kiss. "I'm looking forward to all my family meeting you today."

I simply smiled. I wanted to say I was looking forward to meeting them too, but I had a serious case of butterflies in my stomach.

Christmas Cloches and Corpses

Chapter Twenty-Eight

Jason's grandparents had a beautiful home in Johnson City. I had him carry the banana pudding inside, so I didn't drop it.

"Stop being so nervous," he insisted. "Everyone will think you're terrific."

I'd worn navy wide-leg pants and a checkered blazer à la Katherine Hepburn. I hadn't wanted to show up overdressed, but I'd wanted Jason's family—his parents, in particular—to know I was trying to make a good impression.

I followed Jason into the kitchen where he placed the pudding into the refrigerator.

A woman with shoulder-length silver hair came to kiss him on the cheek. "What have you got there?"

"Banana pudding," he said. "I can hardly wait to dig into it. Granny, this is Amanda."

Granny took my hand in both of hers. "It's a pleasure to meet you. I've heard wonderful things about you."

"Thank you." I smiled. "You have a gorgeous home."

"Aw, now, I can't take credit for that," she said, releasing my hand.

"Yes, she can," Jason said.

"You're right—I can." She laughed. "Take care of her, Jason. The piranha is in a decent mood, but that could change at any second."

"The piranha?" I asked.

"Jason's mom," she said quietly.

"Ah, so you're his *paternal* grandmother."

My observation made her snicker. "Nope, but I know my daughter, and she can be pretty prickly. But she'll warm up to you eventually."

The piranha. That set my mind at ease.

Jason led me through the dining room and the living room, introducing me to people whose names I tried to remember but knew I'd forget. At last, an elegant brunette with perfectly applied makeup turned blue eyes the same color as Jason's on me. The piranha.

"Mom, this is Amanda. Amanda, this is my mom, Peggy."

Peggy Piranha—it was even alliterative.

Extending my hand, I said, "Peggy, nice to meet you."

She briefly shook my hand. "You, too." Turning her attention to her son, she said, "Hi, sweetheart. You look thin. Are you eating enough?"

"I'm eating plenty." He took my hand. "Come on. I want you to meet my dad."

Jason's dad had blond hair and brown eyes. I couldn't see any resemblance between the two of them at all until the man smiled.

Beaming, he reached out and shook my hand. "Hello, there! You must be Amanda. I'm Joshua Logan—call me Josh."

"Nice to meet you, Josh."

I'd barely uttered the words before Jason had to catch me when a child slammed against my legs.

"Careful!" A woman tried unsuccessfully to catch the child. "I'm sorry," she said to me as she passed. "Here, Cody—use your inhaler."

Inhalers, inhalers...does everybody use an inhaler these days?

"Does Cody have asthma?" I asked Jason.

"Yeah, why?" he asked.

"I just wondered. I've encountered three people within the past twenty-four hours who have inhalers. It seems odd, that's all."

Jason's dad retrieved an inhaler from his pocket. "Make it four. I have asthma too."

"That's the thing," I said. "One of the women didn't even have asthma."

Frowning, Josh said, "I don't know why she'd use an inhaler then. Is she a drama queen who maybe wants people to feel sorry for her?"

The words tumbled from my mouth as if they were emerging from my subconscious: "Or it could be she needs an excuse to get into the medicine closet."

"You think someone is using an inhaler to get into the medicine closet at the nursing home?" Jason asked. "Who?"

"Sally Jane. She says she and the nurses put their purses in there to keep residents from getting something harmful." I hated to do it, but I had to. "Jason, I have to leave."

"Of course. Let's go."

"No," I said. "You stay here and enjoy your party. I wouldn't dream of taking you away from it. I can call—"

"Nonsense. Why should you get to have all the fun of exposing a—" He looked around at the children playing nearby. "A bad guy?"

"Your mom will hate me," I said.

"I'll handle her," Josh said. "I can tell this is something important. You two go."

"Thanks, Dad. I'll call you later and fill you in."

On the drive to Winter Garden, I called Grandpa.

"Is the potluck over already?" he asked.

"Not exactly." I explained to him that I had a revelation about Sally Jane. "She told me she volunteers on Saturday, so would you please go stay with Dwight until we get there?"

"Sure. I'm on my way."

After speaking with Grandpa, I called Ryan. My call went to voice mail, so I left him a message setting forth my suspicions.

I ended the call and put my phone back in my purse. I hoped Grandpa or Ryan could get to the nursing home before anything bad happened to Dwight.

At the nursing home, Jason and I hurried inside to the nurses' station. Penelope was manning the desk. Didn't that woman ever get a day off?

"I need to see Sally Jane," I told her.

"Sally Jane isn't here today," Penelope said. "She called in sick."

"Is she diabetic?"

"No." Penelope's face was like a sheet of granite. She was obviously tired of me and my interference.

I glanced down the hall and saw Ryan coming from the direction of Dwight's room. I rushed to meet him.

"How is he?" I asked.

"Dwight is great. He and your grandpa are playing gin rummy," Ryan said.

Looking around to see if Penelope was listening—she was—I said, "I'm sorry for making you come here for nothing. Penelope said Sally Jane isn't diabetic."

"That doesn't mean she isn't up to something shady in the medicine closet," he said. "I'm having my friend, Roger, install a security camera in there first thing Monday." He looked at Penelope, who'd come to linger a few feet away from us. "In the meantime, I want you to keep a log of everyone going in and out. I'm shocked you weren't doing that all along."

Her lips tightened. "Forgive us for trusting our fellow employees." She stormed off toward her desk.

"One thing you learn in law enforcement," Ryan told Jason and me. "Don't trust anyone, especially around drugs or money."

Chapter Twenty-Nine

On Sunday, I was still feeling like an idiot. I'd ruined Jason's party and gotten Grandpa, Ryan, and the nursing home staff in an uproar over nothing. I encouraged Jason to go back to the party, but he wouldn't go. He insisted on staying with me. We wound up shopping for Sienna's gift and a dessert tray for the Secret Santa reveal at Shops on Main.

After feeding Jazzy and getting ready to face the day, I wrapped the presents to take to the Secret Santa party. I'd found a spy kit I thought would be perfect for Sienna. It had rearview glasses, a black light illuminator, a miniature microscope, a fingerprint kit, and a guide to Morse code. I wrapped her gift in paper emblazoned with female superheroes.

I wrapped Ms. Oakes' "home for the holidays" ornament in white paper adorned with silver snowflakes and topped it with an artificial white poinsettia.

Kissing Jazzy on the top of her head, I explained that she couldn't attend the party today because there would be too much chaos in the building. She didn't seem to mind, and I thought she'd be happy having the house to herself for a while. And, yes, as a child, I did watch too many cartoons that gave human characteristics to animals.

I put my packages into the car and drove to Shops on Main. I actually dreaded seeing Jason. By now, his mother would have told him how terrible I was, and he'd know it was true because I'd dragged him away from his grandparents' party for no reason. If he'd told her what had happened, she'd be convinced I made it up in order to get out of there. I mean, sure, I was nervous, but I wouldn't have come up with an excuse to duck out of the family party.

Pulling into the Shops on Main lot, I saw several vehicles, but Jason's wasn't one of them. I was glad I got there ahead of him.

I went inside hoping for a pep talk from Max, but she wasn't there. I'd have thought she'd love being around the festivities, but then I thought she must've spent most of the night watching over Dwight again. I was sick of the way this entire week had gone. Maggie was angry with me and might never let me see Zoe again. I'd falsely accused Sally Jane of tampering with medicines at the nursing home. And I'd ruined my chances of making a good impression on Jason's parents. What else could go wrong?

Connie greeted me in the foyer with a warm hug. "Hi, there! Don't you look beautiful?"

"Oh, Connie, I messed up so badly yesterday." I told her everything that had happened.

"Now, I'm sure everything will be fine. Everyone makes mistakes, and no one makes a good impression on their boyfriend's parents at their first meeting."

I looked into Connie's lovely, kind face. "Really? You didn't immediately win over Will's parents?" I found that hard to believe.

"No. They found me too bohemian—thought I was a hippie."

Okay, that I could believe. "But they quickly came to adore you."

"I don't think they truly accepted me until I had Marielle," she said. "I guess they decided then that I couldn't be all bad."

"You're wonderful," I said.

"I know that, and you know that, but it took them a while." She smiled. "And Jason's family will come to love you too. Are those his parents?"

I froze and felt my eyes nearly bug out of my head. "What?"

"He's walking in with a couple who could be his parents."

I closed my eyes.

"Open your eyes, straighten your back, plaster on your brightest smile, and turn around," she instructed.

"Do I have to?" I asked.

"Yes." She took me by the shoulders and turned me around.

Yep. There was Jason, Peggy, and Josh coming through the door. I faked a toothpaste commercial smile that would've made any beauty queen proud.

"Hello!" I managed to convince my legs to uproot from the spot where I was standing and move forward. "Jason, how wonderful that you've brought your parents." I introduced the Logans to Connie.

While the three of them were exchanging pleasantries, Jason sidled over to me and said, "Surprise."

"It sure is." The smile was beginning to make my face hurt, but I didn't dare let my real feelings show—you know, panic, fear, resentment toward Jason for not letting me know his parents would be coming.

"After yesterday's fiasco, I wanted my parents to—"

"To see me in a better light?" I interrupted.

"I wouldn't have put it like that, but…yeah."

Josh came over to us. "Amanda, that banana pudding was some of the best I'd ever tasted. I hope you'll share the recipe with Peggy."

"Yeah, no problem. I'll send it by Jason."

"And we'll send your bowl back." Josh grinned. "I took the leftovers home with us and made myself sick finishing them off."

"I'm glad you enjoyed it." I saw that Peggy was still conversing with Connie while glaring at me. If Connie couldn't soften the woman toward me, no one could.

Ford and Sienna arrived, and she launched herself at my waist.

"Uncle Ford said you had a present for me!"

"I do." Glad for something to do other than endure the awkward situation with Jason and his parents, I went to the tree where I'd put her gift.

She took it from me. "May I open it now?"

"Let's wait until everyone else gets here," Ford said.

Peggy Logan still hadn't said anything to me by the time Frank, Ella, and Ms. Oakes arrived. I decided to take the initiative to speak with her first.

"Ms. Logan, that's a lovely sweater," I said. "I apologize again for having to leave your mother's party yesterday."

"Thank you." Her face remained stony.

I tried again. "There are some yummy desserts in the kitchen."

"Are desserts all you make?" she asked.

I didn't correct her assumption that I'd made the desserts. "No, but I'm not terribly handy in the kitchen. Would you like to see some of my fashions?"

"Maybe later—after the party."

Ms. Oakes instructed us to join her in the kitchen where there were a variety of crudites, charcuterie, and cheeses in addition to the desserts I'd brought. Everyone couldn't fit into the kitchen at once, and we spilled out into the hallway.

"Thank you all for coming to this little celebration of Christmas and our success here at Shops on Main," Ms. Oakes said, lifting a cup of punch. "I wish you all many blessings over the holiday season and the year to come."

We all echoed Ms. Oakes' sentiment in our own way, and then we filled our plates. Frank realized there wasn't any Christmas music playing, and he hurried to turn it on. I knew I should try to schmooze with Jason's parents some more, but I took my plate and wandered into the lobby where Sienna was looking at the tree.

Smiling, I sat on a bench. "Aren't you eating?"

"Nah, I'm not really hungry," she said.

"You're too curious to know what you'll find in that package," I said.

She grinned. "I'll get something in a few minutes."

I got up, sat down my plate, and retrieved the gift. "Open it."

Eyes widening, she asked, "Are you sure?"

"I'm sure."

Sienna carefully unwrapped her present, and we were both delighted when she saw what it was.

"Amanda, this is awesome!" She sat it down long enough to give me a hug. "I love it!" Grabbing up the spy kit, she hurried down the hall. "Uncle Ford, look!"

Jason came and put his arm around me. "I knew she'd love it."

I laughed. "I'm glad she did. I'd kinda love to play with it with her."

"Don't you mean detect?" he asked.

"Oh, yeah, of course."

Ms. Oakes came into the foyer. "It appears Ms. Tucker feels the party isn't moving along fast enough."

Great. I feel bad enough about ruining Jason's party yesterday. Now Ms. Oakes is calling me out like I'm an unruly schoolgirl. Way to paint me in a good light, Ms. O!

"Sienna wasn't eating, and I wanted her to have her gift," I said, feeling lamer by the minute.

"Well, we might as well open the rest then," Ms. Oakes said. She went to the tree and began handing out the presents.

I received a set of watercolor pencils from Frank, and I went over to thank him. "I love these."

"You're ever so welcome. I'm glad you like them," he said. "Our spy said your coloring pencils were getting a little short." He looked around. "Where'd she go anyway?"

Looking around, I didn't see Sienna. "Let me check in the kitchen."

I went into the kitchen to see Sienna standing against the counter. She had her hands clenched at her sides and her eyes were wide and frightened.

"Sienna, what's wrong?"

Almost before I could finish the question, Sally Jane stepped into the doorway. She was holding a small revolver. "I thought you were a good person, but you're like everybody else. You don't care that insulin my mother needs is being wasted on dying people—or, worse, discarded."

"Surely, there's some sort of agency that—"

"Shut up," Sally Jane said. "You and I are going on a little trip."

"I don't think so," I said.

"Cause a fuss, and I'll shoot everybody in this place— or at least six of them—and I'll start with the girl." She waved the gun toward the hallway. "Now, move."

"How do you think you can get away with this?" I asked. "All those people are going to see us."

"No, they're not. The girl is going to distract them." She turned to Sienna. "Go over there and distract those people somehow, or I'm going to shoot Amanda."

"What should I do?" Sienna wailed.

"I don't know—turn the tree over or something."

Sienna went to the foyer. "H-hey, look at me! I'm going to...to turn over the tree...or something!"

"You're gonna what?" Ford asked.

There was the cacophony of voices speaking at once, and Sienna was sobbing.

"Get ready to move," Sally Jane said, her voice barely above a hiss.

I stared down at the gun and saw a sliver of red on the barrel. When she'd painted it, she'd missed a spot. Fake inhaler. Fake gun. I raised my left elbow and brought it up into Sally Jane's face. I connected and whirled to face her.

Sally Jane screamed as she crumpled to the floor with her face in her hands.

I heard Connie exclaim, "Yes, there is a strange lady in the kitchen! Go see who it is, Trish!"

By the time Ms. Oakes got to us, I had restrained Sally Jane with trash bag ties. Blood from her nose was dripping onto the linoleum floor.

"Could you please call 9-1-1?" I asked.

Ms. Oakes nodded but still stood gaping at me.

"If you don't have your phone handy, mine is in my pocket," I said. "I'm afraid to let go of her wrists because I don't know how long these trash bag zip ties will hold."

She nodded again. "I-I'll get my phone."

Spinning around, Ms. Oakes almost collided with a young woman who I could only guess was Krista—

because why not? It wasn't bad enough that Jason's parents would now be convinced I was a walking nightmare, I was going to make an indelible impression on the building manager's daughter as well.

"Dang, blame it!" Max exclaimed from behind my right shoulder. "What in the world did I miss?"

Epilogue

Maggie dropped Dwight and Zoe off at my house on Christmas Eve. After Sally Jane confessed to putting allergy medication in Dwight's cake, Maggie had apologized for accusing me of doping him, but she apparently felt too awkward around Grandpa and me to stay for our party. I wasn't convinced she wasn't still holding a grudge.

Ryan had discovered that Sally Jane had been bringing two syringes into the medicine closet, one empty and one filled with water. She'd fill the empty syringe with insulin, replace the insulin with water, and hide both syringes in her purse. Then she'd use allergy medicine to sedate the patient whose insulin she'd watered down, thinking they wouldn't need as much medication if they were sleeping. When Clarence Perkins, the nurse's father, had died with a full bottle of insulin, Sally Jane took it believing she could give the other diabetic residents a break while still caring for her mother.

The whole situation was sad, and I was sorry Maggie still hadn't come around enough to spend Christmas Eve with us, but I was glad that meant we could enjoy our time with Max.

Dwight and Zoe followed me into the living room where Grandpa and Max, via video chat, were waiting for us. Grandpa stood and shook Dwight's hand before giving Zoe a hug.

"Your tree is so big and pretty," Zoe said.

"It is awfully nice," Dwight said, "but ours will be just as beautiful next year. Wait and see."

"I like our tree now," Zoe said. "Just because you've come into a little money doesn't mean everything has to be bigger and fancier."

Dwight chuckled. "I like big and fancy. I've waited all my life for big and fancy."

Grandpa laughed. "Speaking of big and fancy, do we want to eat dinner first or open presents?"

"Presents!" Max yelled.

"Since I'm keeping dinner warm in the oven, let's start by letting Max open her gifts first," I said.

"I'm looking at the only gifts I need," Max said. "And I'm pleased as punch that my sweet nephew isn't living in that old folks' home anymore."

It was true—Dwight had moved in with Maggie and Zoe the day the auctions ended. Right now, he was sleeping in Zoe's room while she bunked on the sofa, but he'd made arrangements with Deputy Hall's friend, Roger, to build onto the house as soon as possible. I was happy they were staying close.

"We might be the only gifts you need," Zoe told Max, "but we're not the only ones you've got. Open your email."

"How?" Max folded her arms. "Won't I cut you off? Are you all trying to get rid of me so you can enjoy Christmas without me?"

"Aunt Max, how could anybody enjoy Christmas without you?" Dwight asked.

"I have no idea, darling, but people have been doing it for years."

"You won't cut us off," I said. "Just open a new tab."

"And if you do happen to lose us, we'll be right here when you click back over," Grandpa said.

When she came back to us, Max was laughing.

"This is the best Christmas ever!" she declared. "Thank you all so much for the books, the movies, and the music. Can you hear it?"

"No," Zoe said. "Tell me what song you're playing, and we can play it here too."

"*You're the Cream in My Coffee.*" Max stood and began doing the Charleston as she sang along with the song.

Grandpa got up and offered me his hand. "We can't let her have all the fun."

And that's how four silly people and one goofy ghost celebrated Christmas by dancing around with the utmost confidence that we were all the elephant's eyebrows.

Author's Notes

Thank you kindly!

Thank you for taking the time to read this book. I'm grateful for your support and encouragement. Below are some links to things referenced throughout *Christmas Cloches and Corpses:*

A Pretty Girl Is Like A Melody

https://youtu.be/uVip_kTtxq0

Babe Ruth

Did Babe Ruth ever really visit Bristol? Yes, he did! Major League baseball players used to play exhibition games in some cities as they traveled by train north from spring training to open the season. You can read all about it in this article by Tim Hayes: https://heraldcourier.com/sports/history-with-hayes-the-day-babe-ruth-came-to-bristol/article_d3794e24-76ce-11ea-a7c4-0b1ca2721d55.html And given the Bambino's reputation for being a ladies' man, it isn't hard to believe he'd have flirted with our ghostly fashionista, Max.

Tobacco Baseball Cards

If you're fortunate enough to find a strongbox containing cards from 1909 to 1911, you probably have some treasure on your hands! Find out more at https://www.baseball-almanac.com/treasure/autont005.shtml and https://en.wikipedia.org/wiki/T206.

Etsy

I reference Etsy (https://www.etsy.com/) a lot in this book. That's simply because I think it's a wonderful marketplace. You can find almost anything there— even a pattern for a cloche hat or a toucan mug that assures you that "Toucan do it!" or "Toucan do anything!"

Bury Me Beneath the Willow

https://www.youtube.com/watch?v=IEYk4Jg61gM

Bristol Sessions

Birthplace of Country Music Museum

https://www.birthplaceofcountrymusic.org/museum/

1927 Bristol Sessions towards the end of the list of questions:

https://www.birthplaceofcountrymusic.org/museum/plan-your-visit/faqs/

Video series about the Bristol Sessions

https://www.youtube.com/playlist?list=PLbW6mXnoJcAK_waxYyn8FZy_W-r86tNml

Banana Pudding Recipe

Grandpa Dave and Amanda used this recipe from AllRecipes:

https://www.allrecipes.com/recipe/154584/banana-pudding-with-meringue/

Shine On Harvest Moon

https://www.youtube.com/watch?v=0JkHM6SuntQ

You're the Cream in My Coffee

https://youtu.be/cL1Sr7wxqag

ABOUT THE AUTHOR

Gayle Leeson is a pseudonym for Gayle Trent. I also write as Amanda Lee. As Gayle Trent, I write the Daphne Martin Cake Mystery series and the Myrtle Crumb Mystery series. As Amanda Lee, I write the Embroidery Mystery series. To eliminate confusion going forward, I'm writing under the name Gayle Leeson only. My family and I live in Virginia near Abingdon, Virginia, and I'm having a blast with this series.

If you enjoyed this book, Gayle would appreciate your leaving a review. If you don't know what to say, there is a handy book review guide at her site (https://www.gayleleeson.com/book-review-form). Gayle invites you to sign up for her newsletter and receive excerpts of some of her books: https://forms.aweber.com/form/14/1780369214.htm

Social Media Links:
Twitter:

https://twitter.com/GayleTrent

Facebook:

https://www.facebook.com/GayleLeeson/

BookBub:

https://www.bookbub.com/profile/gayle-leeson

Goodreads:

https://www.goodreads.com/author/show/426208.Gayle_
Trent

Have you read the first book in the Ghostly Fashionista series?

Excerpt from *Designs on Murder*

Chapter One

A flash of brilliant light burst from the lower righthand window of Shops on Main, drawing my attention to the FOR LEASE sign. I'd always loved the building and couldn't resist going inside to see the space available.

I opened the front door to the charming old mansion, which had started life as a private home in the late 1800s and had had many incarnations since then. I turned right to open another door to go into the vacant office.

"Why so glum, chum?" asked a tall, attractive woman with a dark brown bob and an impish grin. She stood near the window wearing a rather fancy mauve gown for the middle of the day. She was also wearing a headband with a peacock feather, making her look like a flapper from the 1920s. I wondered if she might be going to some sort of party after work. Either that, or this woman was quite the eccentric.

"I just came from a job interview," I said.

"Ah. Don't think it went well, huh?"

"Actually, I think it did. But I'm not sure I want to be doing that kind of work for...well...forever."

"Nothing's forever, darling. But you've come to the right place. My name's Max, by the way. Maxine, actually, but I hate that stuffy old name. Maxine Englebright. Isn't that a mouthful? You can see why I prefer Max."

I chuckled. "It's nice to meet you, Max. I'm Amanda Tucker."

"So, Amanda Tucker," Max said, moving over to the middle of the room, "what's your dream job?"

"I know it'll sound stupid. I shouldn't have even wandered in here--"

"Stop that please. Negativity gets us nowhere."

Max sounded like a school teacher then, and I tried to assess her age. Although she somehow seemed older, she didn't look much more than my twenty-four years. I'd put her at about thirty...if that. Since she was looking at me expectantly, I tried to give a better answer to her question.

"I want to fill a niche...to make some sort of difference," I said. "I want to do something fun, exciting...something I'd look forward to doing every day."

"And you're considering starting your own business?"

"That was my initial thought upon seeing that this space is for lease. I love this building...always have."

"What sort of business are you thinking you'd like to put here?" Max asked.

"I enjoy fashion design, but my parents discouraged me because—they said—it was as hard to break into as professional sports. I told them there are a lot of people in professional sports, but they said, 'Only the best, Mandy.'"

Max gave an indignant little bark. "Oh, that's hooey! But I can identify. My folks never thought I'd amount to much. Come to think of it, I guess I didn't." She threw back her head and laughed.

"Oh, well, I wish I could see some of your designs."

"You can. I have a couple of my latest right here on my phone." I took my cell phone from my purse and pulled up the two designs I'd photographed the day before. The first dress had a small pink and green floral print on a navy background, shawl collar, three-quarter length sleeves, and A-line skirt. "I love vintage styles."

"This is gorgeous! I'd love to have a dress like this."

"Really?"

"Yeah. What else ya got?" Max asked.

My other design was an emerald 1930s-style bias cut evening gown with a plunging halter neckline and a back panel with pearl buttons that began at the middle of the back on each side and went to the waist.

Max caught her breath. "That's the berries, kid!"

"Thanks." I could feel the color rising in my cheeks. Max might throw out some odd phrases, but I could tell she liked the dress. "Mom and Dad are probably right, though. Despite the fact that I use modern fabrics—some with quirky, unusual patterns—how could I be sure I'd have the clientele to actually support a business?"

"Are you kidding me? People would love to have their very own fashion designer here in little ol' Abingdon."

"You really think so? Is it the kind of place you'd visit?" I asked.

"Visit?" Max laughed. "Darling, I'd practically live in it."

"All right. I'll think about it."

"Think quickly please. There was someone in here earlier today looking at the space. He wants to sell cigars and tobacco products. Pew. The smell would drive me screwy. I'd much rather have you here."

Hmm...the lady had her sales pitch down. I had to give her that. "How much is the rent?"

"Oh, I have no idea. You'll find Mrs. Meacham at the top of the stairs, last door on your left. It's marked OFFICE."

"Okay. I'll go up and talk with her."

"Good luck, buttercup!"

I was smiling and shaking my head as I mounted the stairs. Max was a character. I thought she'd be a fun person to have around.

Since the office wasn't a retail space like the other rooms in the building, I knocked and waited for a response before entering.

Mrs. Meacham was a plump, prim woman with short, curly white hair and sharp blue eyes. She looked at me over the top of her reading glasses. "How may I help you?"

"I'm interested in the space for rent downstairs," I said.

"You are? Oh, my! I thought you were here selling cookies or something. You look so young." Mrs. Meacham laughed at her own joke, so I faked a chortle to be polite. "What type of shop are you considering?"

"A fashion boutique."

"Fashion?"

"Yes, I design and create retro-style fashions."

"Hmm. I never picked up sewing myself. I've never been big on crafts." She stood and opened a file cabinet to the left of her desk, and I could see she was wearing a navy suit. "Canning and baking were more my strengths. I suppose you could say I prefer the kitchen to the hearth." She laughed again, and I chuckled along with her.

She turned and handed me an application. "Just read this over and call me back if you have any questions. If you're interested in the space, please let me know as soon as possible. There's a gentleman interested in opening a cigar store there." She tapped a pen on her desk blotter. "But even if he gets here before you do, we'll have another opening by the first of the month. The web designer across the hall is leaving. Would you like to take a look at his place before you decide?"

"No, I'd really prefer the shop on the ground floor," I said.

"All right. Well, I hope to hear from you soon."

I left then. I stopped back by the space for lease to say goodbye to Max, but she was gone.

I went home—my parents' home actually, but they moved to Florida for Dad's job more than two years ago, so it was basically mine...until they wanted it back. I made popcorn for lunch, read over Mrs. Meacham's contract, and started crunching the numbers.

I'd graduated in May with a bachelor's degree in business administration with a concentration in marketing and entrepreneurship but just couldn't find a position that sparked any sort of passion in me. This morning I'd had yet another interview where I'd been overqualified for the position but felt I had a good chance of getting an offer...a low offer...for work I couldn't see myself investing decades doing.

Jasmine, my cat, wandered into the room. She'd eaten some kibble from her bowl in the kitchen and was now interested in what I was having. She hopped onto the coffee table, peeped into the popcorn bowl, and turned away dismissively to clean her paws. She was a beautiful gray and white striped tabby. Her feet were white, and she looked as if she were wearing socks of varying lengths—crew socks on the back, anklets on the front.

"What do you think, Jazzy?" I asked. "Should I open a fashion boutique?"

She looked over her shoulder at me for a second before resuming her paw-licking. I didn't know if that was a yes or a no.

Even though I'd gone to school for four years to learn all about how to open, manage, and provide inventory for a small business, I researched for the remainder of the afternoon. I checked out the stats on independent designers in the United States and fashion boutiques in Virginia. There weren't many in the Southwest Virginia region, so I knew I'd have something unique to offer my clientele.

Finally, Jazzy let me know that she'd been napping long enough and that we needed to do something. Mainly,

I needed to feed her again, and she wanted to eat. But I had other ideas.

"Jazzy, let's get your carrier. You and I are going to see Grandpa Dave."

Grandpa Dave was my favorite person on the planet, and Jazzy thought pretty highly of him herself. He lived only about ten minutes away from us. He was farther out in the country and had a bigger home than we did. Jazzy and I were happy in our little three-bedroom, one bath ranch. We secretly hoped Dad wouldn't lose the job that had taken him and Mom to Florida and that they'd love it too much to leave when he retired because we'd gotten used to having the extra space.

I put the carrier on the backseat of my green sedan. It was a cute car that I'd worked the summer between high school and college to get enough money to make the down payment on, but it felt kinda ironic to be driving a cat around in a car that reminded people of a hamster cage.

Sometimes, I wished my Mom and Dad's house was a bit farther from town. It was so peaceful out here in the country. Fences, pastureland, and cows bordered each side of the road. There were a few houses here and there, but most of the land was still farmland. The farmhouses were back off the road and closer to the barns.

When we pulled into Grandpa Dave's long driveway, Jazzy meowed.

"Yes," I told her. "We're here."

Grandpa Dave lived about fifty yards off the road, and his property was fenced, but he didn't keep any animals. He'd turned the barn that had been on the land when he and Grandma Jodie bought it into a workshop where he liked to "piddle."

I pulled around to the side of the house and was happy to see that, rather than piddling in the workshop, Grandpa was sitting on one of the white rocking chairs on the porch. I parked and got out, opened the door to both the car and the carrier for Jazzy, and she ran straight to hop onto his lap.

"Well, there's my girls!" Grandpa Dave laughed.

It seemed to me that Grandpa was almost always laughing. He'd lost a little of that laughter after Grandma Jodie had died. But that was five years ago, and, except for some moments of misty remembrance, he was back to his old self.

I gave him a hug and a kiss on the cheek before settling onto the swing.

"I was sorta expecting you today," he said. "How'd the interview go?"

"It went fine, I guess, but I'm not sure Integrated Manufacturing Technologies is for me. The boss was nice, and the offices are beautiful, but...I don't know."

"What ain't she telling me, Jazzy?"

The cat looked up at him adoringly before butting her head against his chin.

"I'm...um...I'm thinking about starting my own business." I didn't venture a glance at Grandpa Dave right away. I wasn't sure I wanted to know what he was thinking. I figured he was thinking I'd come to ask for money--which I had, money and advice—but I was emphatic it was going to be a loan.

Grandpa had already insisted on paying my college tuition and wouldn't hear of my paying him back. This time, I was giving him no choice in the matter. Either he'd lend me the money, and sign the loan agreement I'd drafted, or I wouldn't take it.

I finally raised my eyes to look at his face, and he was looking pensive.

"Tell me what brought this on," he said.

I told him about wandering into Shops on Main after my interview and meeting Maxine Englebright. "She loved the designs I showed her and seemed to think I could do well if I opened a boutique there. I went upstairs and got an application from the building manager, and then I went home and did some research. I'd never seriously considered opening my own business before--at least, not at this stage of my career--but I'd like to try."

Another glance at Grandpa Dave told me he was still listening but might take more convincing.

"I realize I'm young, and I'm aware that more than half of all small businesses fail in the first four years. But I've got a degree that says I'm qualified to manage a business. Why not manage my own?"

He remained quiet.

"I know that opening a fashion boutique might seem frivolous, but there aren't a lot of designers in this region. I believe I could fill a need...or at least a niche."

Grandpa sat Jazzy onto the porch and stood. Without a word, he went into the house.

Jazzy looked up at me. *Meow*? She went over to the door to see where Grandpa Dave went. *Meow*? She stood on her hind legs and peered through the door.

"Watch out, Jasmine," he said, waiting for her to hop down and back away before he opened the door. He was carrying his checkbook. "How much do you need?"

"Well, I have some savings, and—"

"That's not what I asked."

"Okay. Now, this will be a loan, Grandpa Dave, not a gift."

"If you don't tell me how much, I'm taking this checkbook back into the house, and we won't discuss it any further."

"Ten thousand dollars," I blurted.

As he was writing the check, he asked, "Have you and Jazzy had your dinner yet?"

We were such frequent guests that he kept her favorite cat food on hand.

"We haven't. Do you have the ingredients to make a pizza?"

He scoffed. "Like I'm ever without pizza-makings." He handed me the check. "By the way, how old is this Max you met today? She sounds like quite a gal."

"She doesn't look all that much older than me. But she seems more worldly...or something. I think you'd like her," I said. "But wait, aren't you still seeing Betsy?"

He shrugged. "Betsy is all right to take to Bingo...but this Max sounds like she could be someone special."

First thing the next morning, I went to the bank to set up a business account for Designs on You. That's what I decided to name my shop. Then I went to Shops on Main and gave Mrs. Meacham my application. After she made sure everything was in order, she took my check for the first month's rent and then took me around to meet the rest of the shop owners.

She introduced me to the upstairs tenants first. There was Janice, who owned Janice's Jewelry. She was of average height but she wore stilettos, had tawny hair with blonde highlights, wore a shirt that was way too tight, and was a big fan of dermal fillers, given her expressionless face.

"Janice, I'd like you to meet Amanda," said Mrs. Meacham. "She's going to be opening a fashion boutique downstairs."

"Fashion? You and I should talk, Amanda. You dress them, and I'll accessorize them." She giggled before turning to pick up a pendant with a large, light green stone. "With your coloring, you'd look lovely in one of these Amazonite necklace and earring sets."

"I'll have to check them out later," I said. "It was nice meeting you."

Janice grabbed a stack of her business cards and pressed them into my hand. "Here. For your clients. I'll be glad to return the favor."

"Great. Thanks."

Next, Mrs. Meacham took me to meet Mark, a web site designer. Everything about Mark screamed thin. The young man didn't appear to have an ounce of fat on his body. He had thinning black hair. He wore a thin crocheted tie. He held out a thin hand for me to shake. His handshake was surprisingly firm.

"Hello. It's a pleasure to meet you, Amanda." He handed me a card from the holder on his desk. "Should you need any web design help or marketing expertise, please call on me. I can work on a flat fee or monthly fee basis, depending on your needs."

"Thank you, but—"

"Are you aware that fifty percent of fledgling businesses fail within the first year?" he asked.

I started to correct his stats, but I didn't want to alienate someone I was going to be working near. I thanked him again and told him I appreciated his offer. It dawned on me as Mrs. Meacham and I were moving on to the next tenant that she'd said the web designer was leaving at the end of the month...which was only a week away. I wondered where he was taking his business.

The other upstairs shop was a bookstore called Antiquated Editions. The owner was a burly, bearded man who'd have looked more at home in a motorcycle shop than selling rare books, but, hey, you can't judge a book by its cover, right?

I made a mental note to tell Grandpa Dave my little joke. As you've probably guessed, I didn't have a lot of friends. Not that I wasn't a friendly person. I had a lot of acquaintances. It was just hard for me to get close to people. I wasn't the type to tell my deepest, darkest secrets to someone I hadn't known...well, all my life.

The brawny book man's name was Ford. I'd have been truly delighted had it been Harley, but had you been expecting me to say his name was Fitzgerald or Melville, please see the aforementioned joke about books and covers. He was friendly and invited me to come around and look at his collection anytime. I promised I'd do so after I got settled in.

Then it was downstairs to meet the rest of the shop owners. The first shop on the left when you came in the door--the shop directly across the hall from mine--was Delightful Home. The proprietress was Connie, who preferred a hug over a handshake.

"Aren't you lovely?" Connie asked.

I did not say I doubt it, which was the first thought that popped into my brain, but I did thank her for the compliment. Connie was herself the embodiment of lovely. She had long, honey blonde hair that she wore in a single braid. Large silver hoops adorned her ears, and she had skinny silver bracelets stacked up each arm. She wore an embroidered red tunic that fell to her thighs, black leggings, and Birkenstocks. But the thing that made her truly lovely wasn't so much her looks but the way she appeared to boldly embrace life. I mean, the instant we met, she embraced me. Her shop smelled of cinnamon and something else…sage, maybe.

"Melba, that blue is definitely your color," Connie said. "By the way, did that sinus blend help you?"

"It did!" Mrs. Meacham turned to me. "Connie has the most wonderful products, not the least of which are her essential oils."

I could see that Connie had an assortment of candles, soaps, lotions, oils, and tea blends. I was curious to see what all she did have, but that would have to wait.

"I'm here to help you in any way I possibly can," said Connie, with a warm smile. "Anything you need, just let me know. We're neighbors now."

Mrs. Meacham took me to meet the last of my "neighbors," Mr. and Mrs. Peterman.

"Call us Ella and Frank," Ella insisted. She was petite with salt-and-pepper hair styled in a pixie cut.

Frank was average height, had a slight paunch, a bulbous nose, and bushy brown hair. He didn't say much.

Ella and Frank had a paper shop. They designed their own greeting cards and stationery, and they sold specialty and novelty items that would appeal to their clientele. For instance, they had socks with book patterns, quotes from famous books, and likenesses of authors.

After I'd met everyone, Mrs. Meacham handed me the keys to my shop and went upstairs. Although my shop wouldn't open until the first of September, she'd graciously given me this last week of August to get everything set up.

I unlocked my door and went inside. I was surprised to see Max standing by the window. I started to ask her how she'd got in, but then I saw that there was another door that led to the kitchen. I imagined my space had once been the family dining room. Anyway, it was apparent that the door between my space and the kitchen hallway had been left unlocked. I'd have to be careful to check that in the future.

But, for now, I didn't mind at all that Max was there. Or that it appeared she was wearing the same outfit she'd been wearing yesterday. Must have been some party!

"So, you leased the shop?" Max asked.

"I did!"

"Congratulations! I wish we could have champagne to celebrate."

I laughed. "Me too, but I'm driving."

Max joined in my laughter. "I'm so glad you're going to be here. I think we'll be great friends."

"I hope so." And I truly did. I immediately envisioned Max as my best friend—the two of us going to lunch together, talking about guys and clothes, shopping together. I reined myself in before I got too carried away.

I surveyed the room. The inside wall to my right had a fireplace. I recalled that all the rooms upstairs had them too. But this one had built-in floor-to-ceiling bookshelves on either side of the fireplace.

"Does this fireplace still work?" I asked Max.

"I imagine it would, but it isn't used anymore. The owners put central heat and air in eons ago."

"Just checking. I mean, I wasn't going to light fire to anything. I merely wanted to be sure it was safe to put flammables on these shelves." I could feel my face getting hot. "I'm sorry. That was a stupid thing to say. I'm just so excited—"

"And I'm excited for you. You have nothing to apologize for. How were you supposed to know whether or not the former tenant ever lit the fireplace?"

"You're really nice."

"And you're too hard on yourself. Must you be brilliant and well-spoken all the time?"

"Well...I'm certainly not, but I'd like to be."

"Tell me what you have in store for this place," she said.

I indicated the window. "I'd like to have a table flanked by chairs on either side here." I bit my lip. "Where's the best place around here to buy some reasonably priced furniture that would go with the overall atmosphere of the building?"

"I have no idea. You should ask Connie."

"Connie?" I was actually checking to make sure I'd heard Max correctly, but it so happened that I'd left the door open and Connie was walking by as I spoke.

"Yes?"

"Max was telling me that you might know of a good furniture place nearby," I said.

"Max?" Connie looked about the room. "Who's Max?"

I whirled around, thinking Max had somehow slipped out of the room. But, nope, there she stood...shaking her head...and putting a finger to her lips.

"Um...she was....she was just here. She was here yesterday too. I assumed she was a Shops on Main regular."

"I don't know her, but I'd love to meet her sometime. As for the furniture, I'd try the antique stores downtown for starters. You might fall in love with just the right piece or two there." She grinned. "I'd better get back to minding the store. Good luck with the furniture shopping!"

Connie pulled the door closed behind her as she left, and I was glad. I turned to Max.

"Gee, that was awkward," she said. "I was sure you knew."

"Knew?"

"That I'm a ghost."

Interested in reading more? Designs on Murder, Book One in the Ghostly Fashionista Mystery Series, only 99 cents - www.ghostlyfashionista.com

Made in the USA
Monee, IL
12 November 2020